KU-536-691

3800 12 012893

HIGH LIFE HIGHLAND

By the same author

Toy Breaker
Anger Man
The God Slayer

Vengeance

Roy Chester

HIGH LIFE HIGHLAND LIBRARIES	
38001201289380	
BERTRAMS	18/02/2013
THR	£19.99
AF	

ROBERT HALE · LONDON

© Roy Chester 2013
First published in Great Britain 2013

ISBN 978-0-7198-0816-6

Robert Hale Limited
Clerkenwell House
Clerkenwell Green
London EC1R 0HT

www.halebooks.com

The right of Roy Chester to be identified as author
of this work has been asserted by him in accordance with the
Copyright, Designs and Patents Act 1988

2 4 6 8 10 9 7 5 3 1

Typeset in 10½/14½pt Palatino
Printed in Great Britain by the MPG Books Group,
Bodmin and King's Lynn

To Edward

PROLOGUE

He stared ahead, knowing that he should act.

Was there ever a time when it wasn't there, looking over his shoulder? Ready to sow the seeds of doubt in his mind and undermine his ability to make decisions? To eat away insidiously at his confidence?

Hard to believe sometimes but yes, there was a time when it hadn't been there. For a moment his thoughts drifted. Perhaps he'd been under too much stress. It had been a long high profile case involving a particularly nasty, but very clever, paedophile. And the investigating team were making precious little progress – until they had the breakthrough when they trapped the paedophile in an old warehouse building. They thought they had him then, but they hadn't known about the young girl he was holding hostage. Not until she appeared at a broken window, held there as a human shield to protect the suspect.

'Free passage out, or the girl dies.' The paedophile sounded confident. In control.

'Sir, the suspect's moving back, and I have clear eyeball on him.' The voice came over the net from one of the armed officers in the ring surrounding the warehouse. 'Shall I take him out?'

Silence. Hesitation.

'Sir?'

'Take him out.' The command was clear. Unequivocal. The single shot snapped through the air, and the suspect went down.

The whole episode had lasted only a few seconds, but to him it seemed to stretch into an infinity of uncertainty. A no man's land where reality was suddenly suspended. A place where he was incapable of making a decision. And he'd felt the perspiration running down his face.

Then, just as suddenly, he was back. And no one even knew he'd been absent. But he knew. And he dreaded being drawn back into that desolate no man's land.

She was cold.

Bitter, bitter cold as the icy water ran down her body in jets. She wanted to cry out but the cold dug into her flesh with brittle claws, making her gasp in agony.

She forced herself to look around. To try and make some sense of what was happening. She seemed to be in the centre of a bright light that radiated outwards in rings until it faded away somewhere beyond the curtain of spray that surrounded her.

And she was naked, exposed to the night air. She tried to move, but there were thick ropes binding her to a metal rod in the centre of the jets of water.

All around her, long twisted shards of glass formed patterns in the light, shimmering as the water cascaded down. Shards of glass everywhere, enclosing her in an ice cold cage.

And she kept on screaming.

1

'OK, Fiona, let's get this straight. At 02.48 last night you were found by a private security patrol naked and tied to the Fountain of Peace in Freedom Square. Right?'

'Yes.'

'The two man patrol had been alerted because the fountain was working and the lights were on. Whereas normally the fountain is closed down after midnight and the lights are switched off. So the first question, what were you doing in the area at that time of night?'

They were in Detective Chief Inspector Falcon's office at Garton Police HQ. Falcon had taken Fiona there after the hospital had checked her for hypothermia and taken samples for a tox screen, and the DCI seemed to be struggling to get his head around the events in the square.

'Fiona, what were you doing in the area?' Falcon repeated the question.

'Sorry.' She made a conscious effort to pull herself together. 'I went there in response to your request, of course.'

'My request?'

'Yes. Someone from Police HQ phoned me on my mobile and said there had been an incident in Freedom Square, and that you wanted me to join you there. Are you saying you didn't make that call?'

'I certainly didn't. But whoever did, must have known your mobile number. So how did they get it?'

'Not difficult. Staff mobile numbers are listed on the departmental web sites at the university.'

'What time was the call to you made?'

'Around half past two.'

'And because we've worked together in the past you assumed that I was bringing you in professionally because of something that had happened in the square?'

'That's right.'

'Did this caller identify themself?'

'Yes, it was a woman, and she gave her name as Sergeant Jean Davies. But the name meant nothing to me.'

'Nor to anybody else on the force, I suspect.'

'The message was a fake?'

'Absolutely.'

'But why? Why put me through all that charade with the fountain?' For a moment her voice started to crack.

'Easy now.' Falcon was starting to worry about her mental state. 'Take me through it from the beginning, at your own pace.' He sat on the edge of his desk, watching her carefully.

'After I received the call, I drove to the fountain.'

'OK, so what happened then?'

'At first I was surprised because there was no sign of anything happening in the square. But someone must have been waiting in the shadows because when I got out of the car I remember being stabbed in the arm with a needle.'

'So you were drugged?' Falcon was probing gently.

'Yes, and we'll know what drug was used when the hospital runs the tox screen.'

'Did you see whoever it was that stabbed you?'

She shook her head. 'They just came up behind me when I reached the edge of the square.' Her hands began to shake uncontrollably then.

Falcon walked over to a filing cabinet in the corner of the office, opened one of the drawers and took out a bottle of whisky and two glasses. He poured a decent shot into each glass and passed one to Fiona.

'Drink this. Sorry it's not brandy. But it'll help.'

Fiona drank some of the whisky and coughed as it bit into her throat. But it brought back some of her composure. Falcon sipped his drink, then placed the glass down on the desk.

'You want to go ahead with the questions now, or would you rather leave it until tomorrow?'Falcon asked.

'Let's go ahead. Isn't it one of your favourite maxims – interview as soon as possible while the details are fresh in the mind?'

Falcon grinned. 'I'm always suspicious when people quote me to myself. But, yes, I did say that. And if you still want to go ahead, I'd like to make it formal. By the book. For both our sakes. You agree?'

'Yes, I suppose so. What happened out there tonight shocked me, and I need to know what's going on. Why should anyone do this to me? And I turned to you for help because we'd worked together in the past.' Her voice started to rise.

'Hey, it's OK. We go back far enough. Friends and colleagues. And of course you can turn to me. So let's take this from the beginning.'

Falcon took Fiona into one of the interview rooms and settled her at the small table fixed to the wall. Then he walked over to a tape recorder on a shelf and broke open a pack of tapes. He placed two into a tape recorder and switched the machine on.

Witness Statement from Fiona Nightingale taken on the eighth of May, 2011. Time, 03.30 hours. Present, Fiona Nightingale, who is a forensic psychologist at Waring Hospital, and Chief Inspector Gary Falcon, Garton CID. Dr Nightingale has been advised that she is not being interviewed as a suspect, and she has declined legal representation.

As Falcon prepared the material for the interview, Fiona looked across at him. As usual he was dressed like a male fashion model in a black designer suit, and charcoal grey shirt with a pale blue tie. His skin was a deep ebony, the features of his face strong under a shaven head. It was true, she thought, they had been friends and colleagues for years now, and she trusted him totally. But it had been several months since she'd last seen him, and she thought he looked strained.

'So tell me what happened from the moment you received the

fake call purporting to come from police HQ?' Falcon said, starting the interview.

Fiona went through everything she remembered. But in truth all she could recall was going to the square, then later coming out of a drug-induced state just before the patrol found her strapped to the fountain. In between there were traces of memory, but nothing with any clarity. She knew there was something there. Something important. But it receded again into the mist as she tried to focus on it. Then it came back again.

'There's something there, Gary. I've just remembered.'

'What is it?'

'I told you I didn't see whoever jabbed me in the arm, and I didn't. But there were two of them. They were behind me, but I was supported on both sides when I was jabbed. So there must have been at least two people involved.'

'Good. That could be a very valuable piece of information.'

'So what now?'

'You're still under the effects of the drug, and I think we've gone as far as we can tonight. So I'll arrange for a patrol car to take you to your apartment, and assign an officer to keep a watch on the place. Then in the morning I'll recommend we set up an investigating team.'

'Isn't that overdoing it a bit?'

Falcon shook his head. 'No. Whatever's going down here, someone's sending out a strong message. In fact...' He hesitated.

'What is it, Gary?

'It looks as if whoever's behind this is tormenting you. Making it clear that they can reach you, but not actually doing you any physical harm – at least, not at this stage. But as to why the charade with the fountain?' He shrugged. 'I've got no idea.'

It suddenly snapped into place in Fiona's mind.

'What is it?' Falcon was appalled at her expression. At the fear in her eyes.

'I've just realized why that charade was staged at the fountain. Think about it. That fountain is made of long shards of glass twisted into strange shapes.'

'So?' Falcon still didn't see it.

'Where else was I in close contact with shards of broken glass?'

'Oh, Christ.' Falcon's voice was a thin whisper. 'In the glass lift. Hanging in the air as the cage disintegrated around you.'

2

When Fiona had left under police escort, Falcon poured himself a coffee from the percolator on a table in the corner of the office. Then he sat down behind his desk, content to let his thoughts drift.

He'd been desperately disappointed not to have been promoted in the recent reorganization of the Crime Management Division of the Garton police. He'd learned that he'd been passed over for promotion from Assistant Chief Constable David Mallory, who had arranged a meeting with Falcon at a pub on the edge of the marshland fringing the estuary. The two of them had worked closely together in the past and they had become friends.

Falcon was well aware of the internal politics that operated within the Garton force. It was the same in all large organisations. But he'd always kept well away from the back biting, empire building cabals that lurked in the shadows at Police HQ. So why had Mallory set-up what appeared to be a clandestine meeting with him?

The ACC was waiting at a table by a large window with a view onto the sweep of marshland. He was a tall, powerfully-built man, casually dressed in sports coat and slacks. His face was best described as craggy, the broken nose a souvenir of his days as a loose forward playing professional rugby league for Garton. When Falcon arrived, Mallory greeted him then walked over to the bar and ordered two pints of bitter which he carried to the table. He handed one of the glasses to Falcon and they sat down.

'Like the old days, with you and me working a case.' Mallory broke the ice.

Falcon grinned. 'I suppose we did spend rather a lot of time in drinking establishments, didn't we?'

'That we did.' Mallory agreed, somewhat wistfully.

'How's Janet?' Falcon asked. Mallory had recently married a vicar with a downtown Garton parish.

Mallory grinned, a smile that lit up his eyes. 'Taking far too much on, as usual. '

'And her back after the operation? '

'It's good. Plays up sometimes, but she can handle it. And Denise?'

It was Falcon's turn to grin. 'As beautiful as ever, and the kids seem to be growing up far too fast.'

Falcon looked across at Mallory and raised his glass. 'To the old days.'

'Yeah, the old days.' Mallory raised his own glass and sighed. 'I used to come here then for the odd unofficial get-together with someone higher up the ladder.'

'Who?' Falcon wondered why Mallory had told him that?

Mallory shook his head. 'You know better than to ask that, Gary. Let's just say he was looking after my interests. And his own as well, if truth be known. Nothing comes free.'

There was an edge of cynicism in Mallory's voice that hadn't been there when they'd worked together. It surprised Falcon because all the years he'd worked with Mallory he'd never suspected him of political wheeling and dealing.

'Wheels within wheels, Gov?'

'It's the way of the world, Gary.' For a moment he didn't say anything else and Falcon had the distinct impression that Mallory was wondering how far he could go. How far he could trust Falcon now? 'It sometimes does no harm to have someone looking after your interests.' Mallory continued. Falcon realized that he was still probing.

'Do my interests need looking after?' Falcon asked.

Instead of answering Mallory went off on a tangent. 'What do you think of the proposed changes to the way the Force is to run?'

'I don't know that much about them. None of the foot soldiers do. We all know changes are in the offing, but they've been kept pretty much under wraps. The only rumour doing the rounds is that Crime Management will get a new superintendent to act as your deputy.'

There. It was out in the open now.

Mallory nodded. 'The proposed changes are all set-out in a position paper that the Chief Constable's been putting around to senior officers. It's called *"The New Face of Modern Policing in the Urban Environment - Responding to Changes in Community Cohesion Trends"*.'

'Jesus.' Falcon grimaced. 'Management speak gone mad.'

'I agree.' Mallory nodded. 'But the implementation of the changes advocated in the paper have now reached the second stage, and have gone out for comment to selected middle management officers. There are two central changes proposed. One is to give more power to the mayor's office and the local community. No problem there, because this slots in with the replacement of Police Authorities, and goes along with the idea of democratically elected Police and Crime Commissioners. The PCCs.'

'And the second change?' Falcon felt a stab of unease.

'Ah, that's different, and in a way much more serious. At least, from the point of view of the day-to-day running of the Garton force. At present, everything revolves around the Senior Management Group, but the idea is to dismantle the group when the PCCs are appointed.'

This was a fundamental far-reaching trend and Falcon took a drink of his beer to give himself a moment to think.

But Mallory cut in. 'So why did I bring you out here to discuss the changes?'

'The thought had crossed my mind.' Falcon felt the excitement. Was he about to be offered the job as number two in Crime Management?

'Like I said, it does no harm to have someone looking after your interests. But this time the news is not good, I'm afraid.'

Falcon looked away. But he was too late to hide his feelings.

'Gary, I know you expected to be promoted to superintendent and take over as number two in Crime Management.'

Yes, he had thought that, Falcon acknowledged silently. 'But it's not going to happen. Is that why you brought me here – to tell me that I won't be promoted to number two in Crime Management?'

'You won't get the promotion, no. All right?' Mallory raised his hands. 'I haven't done much to support your interests so far, true. But until things settle, my influence is limited. Still, we're not quite at the end of the line yet, Gary. Some big changes will be implemented over the next few months. But as you said yourself just now, most of the officers on the force seem to know that the core structure is that I will be head of an enlarged Crime Management Division with a superintendent as my immediate deputy. The point here, as it affects you, is that it was decided some time ago that the deputy was to be appointed from outside the force. Chief Constable's idea. New blood and all that.'

An outside appointment. Falcon could almost feel the knife being turned.

'What's the new man's name?' Falcon said, fighting to hide his disappointment.

'Loxley.'

'I knew Loxley was being interviewed for a job in the Garton force. But I'd no idea it was for the post of deputy in Crime Management. None of us did.'

'I'm sorry, Gary.'

'When does he take up his appointment?'

'The beginning of next week. I understand you're away on a course then.'

'Yes.'

'Well, Superintendent Loxley will be on the books by the time you return.'

'And?'

Mallory hesitated. 'We go back a long way, Gary.'

'I know.'

'So let's just say that I wanted to warn you.'

'Warn me of what?'

'To watch your back. This Loxley has a bit of a reputation.'

'What kind of reputation?'

'According to colleagues who've served with him in the Met,

when push comes to shove our boy Loxley has the reputation of looking after number one.'

'When did you learn this about him? '

'It was after we'd made the appointment. A friend of mine in the Met heard about it and warned me that Loxley came with baggage. But it was all rumour and no real substance.'

'Even so, it was enough to make your friend warn you about Loxley?'

'Yes.'

'So why was Loxley appointed?'

'He'd worked with the Chief Constable who, as you know, also came here from the Met.'

'The Chief Constable was able to swing Loxley's appointment with the Staffing Committee?'

'In all honesty, he didn't have to "swing it", as you put it. No, Loxley's record as an administrator is first class, and he certainly came over very well in his interview. He seemed just the sort of senior officer the chief constable wanted as number two in Crime Management.'

Falcon stood up and walked to the bar. When he returned he was carrying two pints and he passed one to Mallory then sat down.

'Thanks for warning me about Loxley's appointment. It's appreciated.'

Mallory looked away for a moment. 'The old saying, Gary. Forewarned is forearmed. You really don't want to get on the wrong side of Loxley. And if you do cross him, you're going to need all the friends you can find.'

'And will I find these "friends" when they're needed?'

Again Mallory hesitated. 'Let's put it this way, there are a few officers on the force who wouldn't shed any tears if Loxley came a cropper.'

'Why?'

'They're looking to their own empires because there's talk that the chief constable's "golden boy" might be given a second role of *supremo* overseeing the implementation of the changes. And if that's true, it will make Loxley one of the most powerful players on the board – which will not be to everybody's liking.'

Falcon started to say something, but Mallory held up his hand. 'Let's just talk about the old days, shall we? Just two coppers reminiscing about the past.'

When Mallory left, Falcon stayed behind, trying to make sense of the evening. As far as he could work out, the meeting had had two main purposes. First, to tell him he wasn't going to be promoted and second, to warn him about the man who'd actually been given the promotion.

Was that it? Was Mallory simply looking after the interests of an old friend? Fair enough, Falcon thought. That happened all the time.

What disturbed him was that an officer as senior as Mallory had bad-mouthed another senior officer in that way. Even to the extent of saying some on the force would welcome Loxley's fall from grace. Was there something else here, Falcon wondered? Was he being drawn into a political power struggle where the prize was nothing less than shaping the future direction of the Garton force? And was Mallory revealing another side to his character by playing politics?

Sitting in his office, Falcon realized that whatever side issues had emerged from the meeting with ACC Mallory, he would have to work with Superintendent Loxley. And it seemed that their first investigation would be the attack on Fiona. So be it, Falcon thought. At least he'd been warned to watch his back as far as Loxley was concerned.

But he still had no real idea what was happening beneath the surface. And as if all that wasn't enough, problems seemed to be developing between him and his father.

Reluctantly, Falcon brought his thoughts back to the present and phoned the front desk, asking the duty officer to put him through to Loxley's home. Time to put the superintendent in the picture.

3

Even after staying in the shower with the temperature as high as she could stand, Fiona still felt muzzy headed. She considered phoning Falcon and putting off the meeting at Police HQ. But in the end she decided it might as well go ahead, if only because it would focus her mind on the fact that someone had taken the trouble to replicate the incident with the glass lift.

It still gave her nightmares. Trapped in the open air in a glass cage that threatened to break up and lance her body with razor sharp shards of glass. The panic of knowing she couldn't move without the risk of being sliced into shreds. And all the time the dreaded sound of the glass sheets grinding together and starting to snap apart.

As she dressed she forced her mind to concentrate on the day ahead. She had to stay strong, she knew that. But the fear was still there, and now she was beginning to recognize that it had only been hidden underneath a shallow layer of bravado. Were the cracks beginning to now appear, she wondered? Triggered by what happened at the fountain.?

When she'd finished dressing she looked at herself in the full length mirror on the wardrobe door. She was no beauty. She'd always known that, but she was comfortable with the way she looked. Medium height and slim, with a good figure honed by weekly sessions in the gym. Then she glanced at her face, framed in her shoulder length dark hair. High cheek bones, a finely chiselled nose that was tilted at the tip, and a mouth that was really too large. But her eyes? 'Mirrors of the mind', as someone had once described a person's eyes. Did they betray her state of mind, she wondered? She looked closely at her reflection, but failed to detect any tell-tale dark shadows under her eyes.

Maybe she was stronger than she gave herself credit for. But she knew that would be put to the test after the incident at the fountain. Someone out there was gunning for her.

4

Falcon stood up as Loxley came into his office the following morning.

'Gary, thanks for coming in early.' Loxley strode forward and held out his hand.

'No problem.' Falcon looked at Loxley as they shook hands. He was tall, well over six feet, Falcon guessed, with thinning blond hair and blue eyes, and an expression that only just stopped short of being arrogant. And, rather surprisingly for a detective, he was in uniform, the superintendent's badges of office on his shoulders. Was he deliberately making a point, Falcon wondered?

'Can I offer you a cup of coffee?' Falcon asked.

'No thanks, I expect there'll be coffee by the gallon at the meeting I have to attend upstairs.'

'So have a seat.' Falcon waved Loxley to a chair. Then he sat down behind the desk, and waited for Loxley to start.

'Gary, you were away when I took up my appointment, and we haven't had a chance to get to know each other yet. We can catch up on everything later, but at this stage I just wanted to touch base after your phone call last night. So can you run me through what we've got again, please.'

'In the early hours of yesterday morning there was an incident at a fountain in the city centre. A naked female was found strapped to a rod in the fountain, and the water was turned on. But, as I explained over the phone, what made the incident special was that the victim was Dr Fiona Nightingale, a forensic scientist who's sometimes employed as a consultant to the Garton police.'

'Someone playing the revenge game?'

'It's very early stages, but it looks that way.'

'How is Fiona ?'

'Difficult to tell because she was drugged before she was tied to the fountain, and she was still recovering last night. But she appears to be coping.'

Loxley picked up a hint of hesitation in Falcon's voice.

'Are you concerned that what happened at the fountain might leave lasting scars on her mind?'

'I'm not sure, but there is something that could impact on her mental state.'

'And what's that?'

'It seems whoever was responsible for what happened at the fountain was replaying an earlier incident in which Fiona was trapped in a glass liftlift.'

'So it does look like a case of someone getting their own back on Fiona?' Loxley pushed the point again.

'Too early to start assigning a motive to the attack, but I agree that it's already starting to look as if this might be a revenge attack by someone who's got it in for Dr Nightingale?'

'Any name jump to mind?'

'Maybe, but I want to do some checking before I come up with a suspect.'

Loxley nodded. 'Anything else I need to know at this stage?'

'I don't think so. At least, not before the briefing.'

'One other thing.' Loxley said. 'I've agreed a team structure with ACC Mallory, and I'll go over that with you now.'

Loxley ran through the agreed structure, but Falcon was only half listening. Normally, he would have expected Loxley to discuss operational issues with him before taking anything upstairs for official approval. Was this all part of some macho power game to make sure the hierarchy was clearly defined, Falcon asked himself? Or was he being paranoid?

'And by the way,' Loxley said. 'The ACC was very concerned when I told him Fiona Nightingale was the victim here. Does he know her well?'

'Well enough. And they have a lot of respect for each other.'

At that stage Loxley stood up, indicating that the meeting was over. 'I'm glad we've made contact at last, Gary. And I look forward to working with you.'

When Loxley had left, Falcon poured himself a steaming cup of hot coffee and tried to sort out his first thoughts on Superintendent Loxley. Up until the end of the meeting, Falcon's overwhelming impression was that of a senior officer who was quick to get a grasp of the facts, and who was prepared to listen. There were also signs that Loxley could be quick to make it very clear who was boss but that was understandable for a new boy determined to make his mark from the start. Falcon decided that on the question of Superintendent Loxley, the jury was still out.

But for his part, Falcon hadn't been entirely honest with the superintendent because he'd held back on one vital piece of evidence. He hadn't told Loxley he could already identify Fiona's attacker.

Because he knew it was impossible.

5

'The new man in place yet?' Fiona asked Falcon as they waited in the DCI's office to be called for the briefing.

'Superintendent John Loxley, or Robin Hood, as the men already call him.' Falcon replied. 'Yes, he took up his duties a week or so ago.'

'What exactly is the new set-up now David Mallory's moved upstairs as an Assistant Chief Constable?'

'As I understand it, the ACC will run Crime Management with Superintendent Loxley as his number two.'

'And this shake up leaves you where?'

'Where I was. More or less.'

She thought she caught a note of bitterness in his voice.

'Problem, Gary?'

Falcon shrugged. 'They've brought someone in over my head. I'll just have to live with it, I guess.'

'What do you think of Superintendent Loxley?'

Falcon shook his head. 'I've just come back off a course on information sharing, and I only met the super for the first time this morning. We discussed your case, but we haven't worked together yet.'

He left it at that, and Fiona didn't push the matter. But it was obvious something was troubling Gary Falcon.

'So, I'm a case, am I?' she asked, trying to make it sound light. 'Seems strange really, being on the other side of the counter for a change.'

'I can believe it.' Falcon crumbled the styrene coffee cup he was holding and tossed it into a waste bin, thinking that he was drinking far too much coffee these days.

'The super will be here soon,' he said. 'In the meanwhile, he's agreed a team structure with DCC Mallory. For the moment, it's a small team headed by Superintendent Loxley, with me as number two. Dan Logan will run the operational side and Goldilocks will handle data gathering with back-up from her team. But it's flexible, and we can pull in other resources as and when they're needed.'

As if on cue, there was a knock on the door and Sergeant Maltravers came in to the office.

To describe the sergeant as statuesque was an understatement, Fiona thought. She was tall, with a figure to kill for. But there was much more to her than that. She had 'presence'. Innocent blue eyes and long blonde hair which she usually wore tucked demurely into a police hat that on her looked like a designer item. On top of all that, her gentle demeanour and agony aunt persona made her universally popular with both male and female members of the force, throughout which she was known affectionately as Goldilocks. Oh, yes, Fiona thought. She was also a computer genius.

'Hey, babe, I heard what happened last night. Weird.' Goldilocks touched Fiona on the arm in a gesture of sympathy. 'All that was staged for your benefit?'

'It looks that way, yes.'

At that moment the phone on the desk buzzed. Falcon lifted the receiver, acknowledged the call, and put the receiver back.

'That was Superintendent Loxley. He's waiting for us in the operations room.'

Goldilocks rolled her eyes. 'Getting a bit high profile, aren't we'?

Falcon nodded. 'True, it's normally used for major large-scale incidents, but it's free at the moment and it's been assigned to us. Proof of just how seriously the Chief Constable takes the threat to Fiona.'

The operations room was in the basement of the Police HQ. Most of the floor space was taken up by a long table which had a large flat-bed TV and a bank of computers on it, together with an impressive looking communication console. Much of the lower wall space was taken up with whiteboards and metal shelves holding cardboard witness statement boxes. Following a number

of national high profile cases, items of evidence were stored elsewhere in the basement under secure conditions designed to
prevent cross-contamination.

Loxley was waiting in the operations room.

'Fiona, this is Superintendent John Loxley, acting number two in
Crime Management.' Falcon made the introductions.

'Dr Nightingale, I've heard a great deal about your work for us,
and it's a pleasure to meet you. Or at least it would be under other
circumstances. But let me assure you at the start, we're taking this
threat against you very seriously.' His accent was Middle England,
and he sounded very formal.

Fiona smiled. 'Thank you. I appreciate that.'

'And this is Sergeant Maltravers.'

Loxley nodded at Goldilocks. 'We met last week when the
sergeant gave me a tour of her domain. And very impressive it
was.'

'Thank you, Sir.'

'So, I'm the senior investigating officer, with DCI Falcon as my
number two. And I want all members of the team to know from
the start that it's been agreed that any extra resources that are
needed will be made available. End of. We don't take kindly to one
of our own being threatened.'

He turned to Falcon. 'Can you run through what we have so far,
Gary? I want to be certain every member of the team is up to speed.'

Falcon took them step by step through the sequence of events of
the previous night – from Fiona receiving the call asking her to go
to the square, to the moment the security patrol had found her
strapped naked to the fountain with the water running.

Falcon looked around. 'That's what happened in a nutshell. But
we can take things a stage further. The fountain has a special rele-
vance because of Fiona's connection to the glass lift.'

Loxley heard Fiona's sharp intake of breath, and he turned to
her. 'Gary mentioned that, but can you expand on it, please?'

'Let me explain.' Falcon came in before Fiona could answer the
question – as if he was protecting her, she thought. 'It happened in
the most recent case that Fiona helped us with. At the climax, she

was trapped in a shattered glass lift suspended in the air. She was rescued, but she was badly cut.'

'Thank you, Gary.' Fiona smiled at Falcon, acknowledging that she understood he was trying to shield her. 'And we have to face it – whatever's going down here is linked with that incident in the lift. If for no other reason than the fountain they tied me to is made of shards of glass.' She shivered at the memory.

'So they stripped you naked and bound you to the fountain.' Loxley said. 'And before that you were drugged.'

'Yes, I felt a needle plunged into my arm.'

'Silly question to a medic, but are you sure it was a needle?'

'Yes, I'm sure.'

'Do we know which drug was used?' Loxley again.

'No, the tox sceen report hasn't come in from the hospital yet.' Fiona replied.

'OK.' Loxley seem happy to leave the question of the drugs for the moment. 'What sort of fountain is it?'

'Modern art.' It was Goldilocks who answered. 'It's made entirely of glass, and it won a competition to symbolize faith and provide a permanent monument to an international conference on religion that was held here in Garton. In fact, the incident with the glass lift occurred during the conference.'

Loxley nodded and turned back to Fiona. 'So it's probable that what happened at the fountain was a gesture. Something to put the frighteners on you. And to do that they targeted one of your worst fears – being suspended in the glass lift. But – and I think this is important – they did not appear to place you in extreme danger. You agree?'

'Yes.' Fiona nodded. 'It was meant to terrify me. And it bloody well worked.'

'We talking past patients with a grudge?' Loxley asked.

'Not patients. I think we're talking *one* patient with a grudge against Fiona.' Falcon dropped his bombshell. 'Debbie Connelly. The Mad Woman, as the media called her. Except, of course, it couldn't have been her.'

6

'The Mad Woman, who's that? ' Loxley asked Falcon.

'Debbie Connelly. The person who tried to kill Fiona in the lift,' Falcon replied.

'So why did you say it couldn't be her?'

'Because she's still locked away in a secure mental health clinic. And if she'd escaped we would have been informed because this is her home area.'

'What about somebody acting on her behalf? Loxley asked.

'Possible, I suppose.' Falcon didn't sound too enthusiastic.

Goldilocks turned to Loxley. 'Before we go any further let me run a few checks on Debbie Connelly.'

'Go ahead.'

Goldilocks left the room. It was almost half an hour before she returned, and she looked shocked.

'Problems?' Falcon read the expression on her face.

'Sorry I've been so long, but I've been talking to the local police, as well as to the staff at the clinic. DI Falcon's right. Debbie Connelly couldn't be responsible for what happened at the fountain last night, for one very simple reason. She died two days ago.'

'Go on.' Falcon broke the silence.

'It was the old story. Remember she was an actress by profession and she faked an illness, a bad stomach complaint. Apparently, the act was good enough to fool the doctors at the clinic who transferred her to a local hospital for tests. By rights she should have been taken to a prison hospital, but her condition was considered to be an emergency and she got away while she was waiting to be assessed in A&E.'

'So why weren't Garton police informed that she'd gone on the run? Loxley asked Goldilocks.

'It wasn't necessary because Debbie Connelly committed suicide on the day she escaped from the clinic.'

'What were the circumstances?' Loxley asked Goldilocks.

'I've pieced most of the story together using the info I got from the people at the clinic where she was being held, and from the police. The clinic's in Cornwall, and apparently Debbie was a skilled sailor. It seems that on the evening of the day she fled from the hospital she went to a small marina on the outskirts of Penzance and hired a dinghy from a boat rental agency.'

'How did she pay the hire fee?' Falcon asked.

'With a credit card issued in her own name.'

'How do we know that?'

'From the police investigation that started as soon as the marina owner reported the dingy missing.'

'Is it usual for patients at mental health clinics to have cash cards?' Loxley asked.

Fiona shrugged. 'If they go out on supervised shopping sprees, and if they have a bank account, yes, they can take their credit cards with them. In fact, it might well be part of their overall therapy treatment.'

'What else did you learn from the local police?' Loxley asked.

'Debbie Connelly told the man in the marina office that she was an experienced sailor and just wanted to do a bit of sea sailing that evening. He saw nothing wrong and rented her a dinghy until nine o'clock that night. Then she sailed away into the sunset, as it were, and was never seen again. And when she didn't return the dinghy, the alarm was sounded, and a full air sea search was mounted with the Coast Guard and the RAF involved. The splintered dinghy was found later, floating close to a dangerous rock outbreak.'

'And Debbie's body?'

'Not found yet. But apparently that's not unusual because if she'd gone into the water at the spot where the wreckage was found, the currents would have dragged her body out to sea. After twenty four hours the search was called off, and Debbie Connelly's parents were informed. It turns out that she had phoned her mother and father earlier on the evening she committed suicide. She told them how sorry she was for all the trouble she'd put them through over the years, but that they didn't have to worry about her anymore.'

'Did she say she was planning to commit suicide?' Falcon asked.

'Yes. She said she was going to end it all. But she hung-up without telling them where she was. The director of the clinic had already contacted Debbie's parents explaining that she'd escaped, and it was then that they told him about the phone call. And that, as far as we're concerned, was that. Except for one important piece of evidence. Debbie Connelly's life jacket was found in the wreckage, and it had been slashed with a knife. Repeatedly. As if Debbie Connelly was making absolutely certain it would be of no use if she changed her mind.'

'You thinking what I'm thinking.' Loxley looked at Falcon. 'That she faked the whole thing. And now she's on the loose?'

Falcon nodded. 'Otherwise, the fact that Fiona was tied to the fountain just two days after Debbie Connelly escaped would be too much of a coincidence. And I don't like coincidences. So I agree, Debbie Connelly's on the loose, and she's going after Fiona. But why stage the elaborate ploy with the sailing dinghy?'

'To call off the hounds.' Loxley said. 'It looks very much as if Debbie Connelly had all this planned.'

'It looks that way, yes,' Falcon agreed. 'And from what Fiona remembered, there were at least two people who trapped her at the fountain. So if it *was* Debbie Connelly behind the incident, it's beginning to look as if she had help.'

'It certainly does.' Loxley nodded. 'But there's just one small problem there, isn't there. Until two days ago she was being held in a secure mental health unit. And yet within a few hours of escaping she's staged a suicide, moved from Cornwall to Garton, and set-up the incident at the fountain.'

'So?' Falcon probed.

'So setting all this up would have taken time. Certainly more than two days. No, what happened at the fountain wasn't a crime of opportunity. It had obviously been well planned beforehand. But how could Debbie Connelly have set it up while she was still locked away?' Loxley asked.

'Maybe she had visitors.' Fiona said.

'Let me get back to the clinic and check on that.' Goldilocks left the room again.

When she'd gone Loxley turned to Fiona. 'We've no actual proof that Debbie Connelly's behind all this. But it's looking more certain by the minute. So can you obtain a photograph of her?'

'Sure. I can get one from the hospital records.'

'So, what have we got so far?' Falcon asked Loxley.

'Debbie Connelly nailed her colours to the mast when she recreated the incidence with the glass lift. The message was loud and clear. She was putting the frighteners on Fiona. But at that stage, that's all it was. She had Fiona at her mercy, but she let her go. Like a cat playing with a mouse.'

'So if she *is* playing with you, will Debbie Connelly strike again?' Falcon asked.

Fiona shrugged. 'To answer that, we have to get inside Debbie Connelly's mind.'

7

'I made a quick check on Debbie's behaviour patterns at the clinic,' Goldilocks reported back.

'The staff there wouldn't reveal anything that broke the doctor-patient confidentially, but when I explained that we had reason to believe Debbie had staged a fake suicide attempt and that she was a danger to Fiona, they were more forthcoming.'

She referred to a note book. 'It seems Debbie was very much a loner, although she did apparently have one special friend at the clinic who was later transferred elsewhere.'

'Do we have a name for this friend?' Loxley asked

Goldilocks shook her head emphatically. 'That was one piece of information they definitely wouldn't release. Not without a court order. It seems it would infringe the patient's human rights.'

'Was this friend male or female?'

Goldilocks shrugged. 'They wouldn't even release that information. But they did confirm that over the past year Debbie's had no visitors and no mail. She'd even severed all ties with her mother and father, and she wasn't interested in escorted excursions in the community. But she presented no management problems at the clinic and it seems she spent all her time on computer games.'

'Computer games. ' Loxley sounded surprised. 'Do they allow patients to have computers in mental health clinics?'

'It depends.' Fiona said. 'Some clinics do allow it but it's probable that all the equipment will be confined to one work station, and there will be safeguards on which computer functions can be accessed.'

'OK, so we need to identify this friend Debbie Connelly had at the clinic.' Falcon said. 'Even if it means getting a court order.'

'I'll get onto it.' Loxley said. 'But at this stage, it looks as if Debbie Connelly could be a major player. Why should she hold a grudge against you?' He asked, turning to Fiona. 'Tell me about her.'

Fiona paused for a moment, gathering her thoughts. 'Debbie has a mental health condition that results in her having very low self-esteem. All her life she's tried to compensate for it. As a child she took to acting in school plays as a ploy to hide her lack of confidence in herself. In the end, she became an attention seeker. Big time. And she needs to be centre stage in order to feed her craving for attention. So she took up a career in acting, but unfortunately it didn't assuage her demons because she wasn't very good at it.'

'And the incident with the glass lift?' Loxley asked.

It was Falcon who answered. 'Three religious leaders were murdered around the time a conference on Faith in Crisis was being held in Garton. Debbie Connelly provided us with information on one of the murdered men – an Anglican vicar with a parish in a village outside Garton. Debbie claimed a relationship with him, and she started off by helping the police. In fact, she did provide some useful information on the vicar, who'd gone *AWOL* at the time. But then it turned out that Debbie was deeply involved with the religious fanatic who'd committed the murders. But he died, and to remain centre stage Debbie arranged to highjack the closing ceremony of the conference.'

'To what end?'

'To commit ritual suicide.'

'Why did she intend to kill herself?' Loxley asked.

'A combination of factors really, but most of all her behaviour was underpinned by the lack of self-esteem I mentioned a moment ago. I don't know how much she was in love with her boyfriend, but when he died it must have seemed to Debbie to be the last straw. She appears to have given up the will to live then, and she arranged the episode with the lift that resulted in trapping me above the steps of the Catholic cathedral in a glass cage.'

'And why you?' Loxley said.

'I was part of the investigation into the murders, and to Debbie I was the symbol of all the psychiatrists who she believed had messed up her life. So she decided to kill me as well as herself.'

'But you escaped?' Goldilocks leaned across and put an arm around Fiona's shoulders..

'Yes, I escaped, and Debbie was prevented from committing suicide by landing in a safety net held by the fire fighters.'

'Thank you for explaining.' Loxley said. 'I realize it couldn't have been easy to revisit all that. But we know that the incident at the fountain involved two people. So who helped Debbie Connelly?'

'Maybe this friend at the clinic,' Goldilocks said.

'We keep coming back to this friend,' Falcon said. 'But until we have proof that he, or she, was the one who helped Debbie Connelly I think we need to check out all Fiona's patients that might hold a grudge against her.'

Loxley turned to Fiona. 'Have you had any problems with any of your patients recently?'

'Some, yes. It's inevitable in my profession.'

'Can we identify the patients involved?' Falcon asked.

'If we set up a database, we should be able to,' Fiona replied.

'Sergeant, can you get onto that,' Loxley said to Goldilocks.

'Sure, but I'll need Fiona's help with it because she knows where the data's hiding out.'

'No problem,' Fiona replied. 'I don't have any clinics scheduled for today.'

'Sorry to press, but how long will it take?' Loxley asked Goldilocks.

'Hard to tell. Two, three hours maybe, for a first sweep. But it'll be a lot quicker with Fiona guiding us through the records.'

'Right.' Loxley looked at his watch. 'If we reconvene here at say two we can have a working lunch.'

Goldilocks took Fiona to her domain in the basement of the HQ building, and for the next three hours they worked on compiling the database. When the first draft was put together, Goldilocks pulled a memory stick from the computer they'd been using.

'So let's go and report to our lords and masters.'

8

Loxley and Falcon were waiting in the operations room.

'Any joy?' Falcon asked Goldilocks.

'Oh, I think we've made some progress.' She booted up one of the computers and plugged in the memory stick.

'First, we decided we needed a database on all the patients Fiona's been responsible for that have subsequently been released back into the community. Initially, we set our first cut-off at the past five years. That seemed a reasonable place to start and we put together a database on those criteria.'

'What was the source of these data?' Loxley asked.

'Fiona has her own patient records on disc, and I sent an officer to pick up her laptop from her apartment.'

'Do the records cover all your patients?' Loxley asked Fiona.

'Yes, everyone. But the records on some are more detailed than others.'

'Inevitable, I suppose, with medical records. Am I right in assuming that the more interesting the patient, the more data is logged?' Loxley asked.

'That's true, but there was at least a very basic data set on all of them.'

'So how did you interrogate the patient data?' Loxley turned to Goldilocks.

'We were fortunate in Fiona's case because over the last five years, since she came back to the UK from working in the States, all her patients have at some stage been at the Warings Hospital here in Garton.'

'How many were in that category?' Loxley came in again.

'Over the five years, thirty six, and we concentrated on them. First we decided on what basic parameters we needed to slot into the new database, and we began by listing the date they were committed to the hospital, and how long they stayed there.'

Goldilocks booted up the computer and ran her fingers across the keyboard. As she did so a series of names scrolled across the screen.

'There.' She highlighted one column of data. Ten of the patients died while in the hospital, and eighteen of them are still there so both categories were eliminated on the first pass. Which left eight possible candidates, and we pulled up the records on those. They've all been released from the hospital, and sent to less secure units. Four are still in those units, but four of them were eventually considered well enough to go back into the community with a suitable care package.'

'Can you pull up the names of the four patients released back into the community?' Falcon came in.

'No problem.' Goldilocks tapped several keys and a list of four names scrolled down the left of the screen.

'There they are. Just the names at the moment. Three male and one female.'

'Fiona. Can you supply any details on these four patients?' Loxley asked.

'I expected this, which is why I wanted my laptop. So give me a minute or two to prepare.'

She opened the laptop which was lying on the table and booted it up. Then she plugged a memory stick into a USB port on the side. She opened the data on the memory stick, and asked Goldilocks for the names of the four patients. One by one she called them up, then sat back.

For a few minutes Fiona concentrated on the data filling the screen.

'OK, reading down. *Number 1*, Jack Fisher. Child molester. Ineffectual type with difficulties in forming adult relationships. No longer considered a risk to children, but kept on the Sex Register with regular checks. *Number 2*. George Savage. Manic depressive who threatened extreme self-harm. Responded well to medication. *Number 3, Sarah Maxwell*. Serious schizophrenic with voices that told her to attack members of her family. Like many schizophrenics, her condition is under control with medication. And finally, in a special category, we have *Number 4*, Adam Levine. He suffered from a bi-polar condition. '

'Did any of these four patients have particular issues with you?' Loxley asked

'Yes, Adam Levine did.'

'Why did you say he was in a special category?' Loxley asked.

'Because he wasn't a patient of mine. He came to the Warings Hospital to be assessed, and he was only here a matter of days.'

'Then why include him in the list?' Loxley again.

'Because he threatened me. Told me in front of witnesses at the assessment hearing that I was dead meat.'

'But why?'

'He wanted me to recommend his release. But he had problems and my judgement was that he should be sent to a secure clinic for treatment.'

'What kind of problems did he have?' Falcon asked.

'As I said, Adam suffers from a bipolar affective disorder.'

'What exactly is that?' Falcon asked.

'It's also called a manic depressive illness – a condition similar to that suffered by George Savage – and the name gives some idea of what the condition entails. Essentially, it's a brain disorder that causes severe mood swings. Without, at this stage, breaking doctor-patient confidentiality, I can tell you that in Adam Levine's case, the bi-polar condition was combined with some psychotic symptoms, including hallucinations. Before he came for the assessment he'd been treated with medication and cognitive therapy.'

'What's cognitive therapy?' Falcon again.

'Put simply – talking about your condition, often in a group setting.' Fiona answered.

'And had it helped Adam Devine?'

'Not sufficiently for me to recommend his release back into the community, no.'

'Can you remember anything else about him?'

'I'm not sure.' Fiona sounded curiously hesitant.

'In what way, not sure?' Falcon asked.

'You must remember that I only had a few assessment sessions with him. But there was something he was hiding. I'm sure of that. Some part of his personality that was buried too deep for me to reach. Given enough time I might have broken through. But as it was...' She shrugged. 'I passed him on to the secure clinic.'

'What about Adam Devine as a person?' Loxley asked.

'In many ways he was an enigma. On the face of it, he appeared to fit the classic profile of a loner. He was obsessed with a specific interest, in this case computers. He lived alone, and he didn't seem to need friends.'

'So how was he an enigma?' Falcon asked.

'Well, for one thing he came from a traveller background, but although he kept strong ties with the family it wasn't his chosen way of life. For another thing, he was a very presentable young man. Tall, good looking, affable personality. Not the usual profile of a loner nerd. But what made him especially dangerous was that occasionally he'd go on a bender. And that's when he became uncontrollably aggressive and violent. The index offence happened when he savagely attacked the owner of an off-licence who refused to sell him more drink.'

'Was this part of his bi-polar condition?' Loxley asked.

Fiona shook her head. 'No, but if the mood swings and the drinking coincided he could become a very dangerous man.'

'Anything else about him?' Falcon asked.

'He was well above average intelligence, but much of his mind was focussed on the world of his computer. And ever since he was a teenager he'd been a hacker. One of the best it seems, and in his time he'd hacked into some pretty important databases.'

'Why?'

'At first, simply to show that he could. That he had a superior intellect.'

'So it was all for fun?' Goldilocks asked.

'At first, yes. But later he became involved in some high level computer fraud. The police brought charges against him, but the prosecution failed through lack of evidence.'

'And what exactly was his beef with you?' Falcon asked Fiona.

'He didn't believe he had mental health issues, and he blamed me for locking him away. And for putting the brakes on what he thought was to be a very lucrative career as a professional computer hacker.'

'But at one stage he actually threatened you with violence?' Falcon wanted the point clarified.

'As he left the assessment hearing, yes.'

'This assessment hearing. What form did it take?' Falcon asked.

'He was brought to the hospital and I had four two-hour sessions with him. Then there was the formal Mental Health Review Tribunal with medical and legal representatives present. Largely on my recommendation the panel decided Adam Devine should stay in a high security clinic.'

'What about the other names on the list?' Falcon asked.

'No bells ringing for any of them.'

'So what happened to Adam Devine?' Falcon asked.

'I don't know.' Fiona replied. 'I was only called upon to assess him at the hospital where I work. After that he fell off my radar.'

'You didn't identify a suitable clinic for him?' Loxley asked.

Fiona shook her head. 'Not part of my brief. I was only responsible for his assessment.'

'So we need to trace his history from the time he entered the high security clinic. Sergeant?'

'I'll run a trace on him as soon as this briefing's finished.' Goldilocks said.

The discussion was put on hold then as one of the canteen staff brought a trolley into the operations room. She transferred a platter of sandwiches and a bowl of fruit, together with a coffee percolator, several small cartons of milk and styrene cups, to the table.

They'd just about finished lunch when Cathleen Foster, the force Director of Communications – or Press Officer, as most people still called her – came into the operations room. She was in her late-twenties and had an oval-shaped face and short blonde hair. She was severely dressed in a dark business suit, and there was a no-nonsense air about her that suggested the seasoned professional.

She reported to Loxley. 'Something's come up, Superintendent and I thought you'd want to know about it at once.'

'Sounds ominous. Go on.'

'The Press Office had a visit from a reporter a few minutes ago, inquiring if there was an incident last night involving a forensic psychologist, who he identified as Fiona Nightingale, being strapped naked to a fountain in the city centre. It was flagged with me immediately because that information hasn't been released yet.'

9

'Can we contain this?' Loxley asked.

Cathleen Foster shook her head. 'Normally, I'd say it could just be possible. But it might be different this time.'

'Why?' Loxley said.

'Because the reporter's name's Carl Lucas.'

'Carl Lucas, the writer?' Fiona asked.

'Yes.' Cathleen Forster nodded. 'The guy who made his name specializing in writing about serial killers. In fact, he's produced five bestsellers on the subject, and had two popular series on TV.'

'You know him?' Loxley turned to Fiona.

'I've not met him, but I've read some of his work.'

'What do you think of it?' Falcon asked.

'Carl Lucas was trained as a psychologist, so he has more than a passing knowledge of the criminal mind. And he's a good writer – seems to have the ability to put complex ideas in a form that the layman will understand. Which I suppose is why he's a bestselling author.'

'Do I sense a degree of hesitancy in there?' Loxley asked.

'I suppose so.' Fiona replied. 'At first he managed to avoid the sensationalism that blights much of the reporting on serial killers. But latterly he seems to have pampered to the lowest common denominator. As a result, he's become almost a parody of himself. Too much the TV personality and too little the detached scientist.'

Falcon grinned. 'You're not his number one fan, then?'

Fiona smiled back. 'Open mind, Gary. As always.'

'Is he just a writer?' Falcon asked.

'No, far from it. As I said, Carl Lucas was trained as a psychologist, and he's still in practice running a private clinic in London.'

'So he's not your bog standard reporter?' Loxley asked.

Fiona shook her head. 'Absolutely not, he's very much a practising psychologist.'

'And now he shows up here with information on last night's sideshow that was never made public.' Loxley turned to Cathleen Foster. 'So what's the best way of approaching this?'

'It depends entirely on what he wants. But I think we should talk to him. Try and get him on side if we can. But for that, we may have to offer him something?'

'What do you mean? Offer him something? This is a police investigation,' Falcon cut in. 'We don't have to offer anyone anything.'

Loxley thought for a moment. 'You're right, of course, Gary. But the fact is that he already knows about the incident at the fountain. Which means he's been talking to somebody who has inside information. So let's meet him and see why he's here. Maybe he simply wants to help.'

'Call me cynical, but I very much doubt that,' Cathleen Foster said. 'But I suppose we can try. I'll go and fetch him.'

When Cathleen Foster came back, Carl Lucas was with her.

As the Press Officer made the introduction, Fiona studied the visitor. He was tall, and dressed casually in designer jeans and suede jacket. He had what one of Fiona's friends would call hair to die for – a mass of tight blond curls that he wore unfashionably long.

When she was introduced to Carl Lucas, he shook her hand.

'I know your work, Dr Nightingale, and I've quoted you extensively in my books.' It was a compliment, but somehow he managed to make it sound as if he was doing her a favour in even mentioning her work.

'Shall we sit down?' Kathleen Forster led them over to the table, deliberately seating Superintendent Loxley at the head.

'Mr Lucas.' Loxley started to say something, but Carl Lucas held up his hand.

'Carl, please. I don't go much for formalities.'

Was it a deliberate ploy to put Loxley at ease, Fiona wondered? Or a move to take the initiative, maybe? But if it bothered Loxley he seemed content to let it pass.

'Carl it is then. Now, can I ask how you came to link an incident that took place last night at a fountain in Garton to Dr Nightingale? Because we haven't released any details on the incident?'

Lucas nodded, acknowledging that the superintendent had cut straight to the chase. 'I was contacted through my publishers with a message that an incident had occurred that involved Dr. Nightingale.'

'But why should that be of interest to you?' Loxley pushed the point.

Then Carl Lucas dropped his bombshell.

'Because what happened last night was very much the tip of the iceberg. You see, my information is that the incident at the fountain is going to lead to the exposure of a serial killer. Maybe the worst ever to emerge in the UK.'

10

There was a long silence in the room.

Finally, Falcon broke the spell. 'This message sent to your publisher – what exactly did it say?'

Carl Lucas shrugged 'Come on, superintendent, time to show a few cards. What do I get out of this?'

'What do you want?' Loxley tossed the question back at Carl Lucas. 'You're not a "run of the mill" reporter with deadlines to meet.'

'I want a deal,' Lucas said.

'What kind of a deal?' Loxley asked.

'Whoever sent the message obviously believes that as part of your investigation into the events that started at the fountain, you will uncover evidence of a serial killer. So the deal is this. My contact, the person who sent the message, will supply me with evidence that will expose the serial killer, evidence that will I pass on to you, in exchange for exclusive information on the day-to-day running of your investigation, information that will form the background for my next book.'

So that was it, Fiona thought. Access to the inside story of the hunt for a serial killer.

'The message sent to your publishers' Fiona asked Lucas. 'Do you have it with you?'

'I have a copy, yes. The original's in a safe in my editor's office at the publishers.'

Carl Lucas took a sheet of paper from one of his pockets and started to read the message aloud.

Dear Mr Lucas,

You have a reputation as a crime writer specialising in serial killers, and you have written several bestsellers on the topic. I want to offer you the opportunity to write another. But this time, you will be on the inside of the investigation. At the very centre of things.

Think of that.

And the game has already started. It kicked off with an incident at the fountain in Garton involving Fiona Nightingale who is a forensic psychiatrist. And there will be more. Much more, as you unmask one of the most terrible serial killers this country has ever seen. A killer lurking on the streets of Garton. To expose this killer, I will supply you with information that you can pass on to the police. But this will come at a price because the police must agree to allow you to follow the investigation as it develops.

You will be the 'Janus Man', looking both ways at once. A unique position that I don't think has ever been given to a writer before.

And for good will I will give you a titbit of information to prove my inside knowledge. Fiona Nightingale has already been exposed at the crystal fountain. Next, she will step outside the pale and become the subject of a major police hunt. But it could be too late for Fiona as the evidence against her begins to stack up. Evidence that will lead you to the serial killer and shock you to the core.

Poor little Fiona.

11

'I'm sure you understand that we need to talk about this among ourselves.' Loxley faced Carl Lucas.

'Yes, I understand that.'

'So I'm going to ask Sergeant Maltravers to take you for a coffee in the canteen while we decide on our position.'

When they'd left Loxley turned to Falcon. 'Let's look at the means of communication first. The original letter and envelope are in the publisher's safe, but it might be worthwhile getting them both checked out for a DNA profile. You never know, whoever sent it might have licked the flap. Not probable, but worth a shot. Now, what do you make of the letter itself?'

Falcon shrugged. 'I really don't know. I've never come across anything quite like it. A criminal who's prepared to furnish a writer with information to pass on to the police, providing the writer's allowed inside an on-going investigation. My first thought would have been, no way. I would have said that whoever wrote that letter has got to be a nut case. Except.'

'Except? ' Loxley asked.

'Except for the information about the incident at the fountain. It didn't come from us.'

'So what are you saying? That maybe whoever wrote the letter *can* actually supply us with genuine evidence?'

'I don't know. But I don't think we can afford to just sit back and ignore evidence that comes in from a source that's already proved it's reliable – even if that evidence is wrapped up in bloody riddles.'

'Riddles.' Loxley repeated the word. 'The letter can certainly be viewed on a number of levels. For a start, there's the suggestion that we will expose a major serial killer as our investigation proceeds. Then there's the warning that Fiona will step outside the pale and go on the run.' He turned to Fiona. 'What's your take on that?'

She shook her head. 'Frankly, I don't know what to think.'

Falcon sensed the fear in her voice. 'We can't ignore the letter, I agree. But we can keep Fiona under wraps and shield her from danger.'

It was a symptom of Fiona's state of mind that she didn't argue with Falcon.

'OK, that's agreed. We keep Fiona safe,' Loxley said. 'But let's look at this from another point of view for a moment. Why should whoever wrote that letter *want* to supply Carl Lucas with information that will be vital to a police investigation?'

'To be at the centre, playing the "Ring Master." It was Fiona that answered, and her voice was bleak. 'It's one more piece of evidence that suggests all this is down to Debbie Connelly. The quintessential attention seeker. And bringing in Carl Lucas is a master stroke because the book that he is expected to write will be Debbie Connelly's testimony. An ego trip inside a bestseller.'

'Whichever way we turn, we keep coming back to Debbie Connelly,' Falcon said.

'True,' Loxley agreed. 'But right now we need to clarify the position of Carl Lucas. We seem to be in agreement that we can't afford to ignore him. Particularly since the letter writer has promised to supply further information to us via him. And that information might connect to a serial killer here in Garton. So how do we handle Lucas?'

'Treating him as a police witness providing us with information is one thing,' Falcon said. 'Giving him full access to an investigation is another. But I suggest we use him for our own ends. Let him bring us anything the letter writer gives him? In exchange he can watch the investigation unfold. But we keep him on a very tight rein, and be selective in what we feed him. He must expect that anyway.'

'But what about his status?' Falcon persisted. 'This has to be clearly defined. For our sake as well as his. Everything has to be squeaky clean and above board these days. Particularly if Lucas has to give evidence in court later. So how do we define his role?'

'Perhaps I could make a suggestion,' Kathleen Forster answered.

'Go ahead.' Loxley replied.

'The best way forward could be to make everything official from the start, and to do that you treat him as a police informant, or a "covert human intelligence source", to use the modern jargon. As you're well aware, after the good old days when almost anything went, the use of informants is now governed by strict protocols. Using Carl Lucas in the category of an informant, which in a sense he already is since he came to us with information, would put him the same category as someone who had infiltrated a criminal organisation. And it would allow you to discuss aspects of the investigation with him. Openly and on the record. And, of course, you can withdraw your co-operation with him at any time, if he fails to come up with the goods.'

'Gary? You seemed to have doubts about bringing Lucas on board.'

'I did, but I'll settle for treating him as an informant. If for one reason only.'

'And what's that?' Fiona asked him.

'I don't like loose cannons, and to paraphrase a certain American statesman, I'd rather Lucas was "on the inside of the tent pissing out, than on the outside pissing in".'

12

Carl Lucas was happy to play the role of police informant so long as it kept him in the inner circle, and he readily agreed not to reveal anything he learned until the investigation was over. To back this up he pointed out that it was in his own interest to keep everything exclusive for the book he intended to write.

On a practical level, it was agreed that he would be given access to members of the investigation team. But it had been made very clear that he would not be allowed to be present at official briefings unless invited to attend by either Loxley or Falcon.

Under those constraints, Falcon had been briefing Lucas, bringing him up to speed with the investigation. And because the team was still assessing the importance of the letter, Lucas was allowed to attend the next briefing meeting.

Loxley opened proceedings. 'According to the letter sent to Carl Lucas's publishers, our investigation will expose the work of a serial killer – one of the worst ever to emerge in the UK. How much credence do we put on that?'

'It's certainly a show stopper.' Falcon was the first to reply. 'And it was obviously thrown into the mix to grab our attention. Of course, that doesn't mean that the serial killer's not real. But I suggest that for the moment we let that part of the investigation develop at its own pace. At least, until we have real proof that the serial killer actually does exist. Meanwhile I suggest we concentrate on the attack on Fiona.'

'Wait a minute.' Loxley held up a hand. 'According to the letter sent to Carl, Fiona and the serial killer are somehow linked to each other. Right?'

'They might be connected, yes. But I don't want to take the spot-light off Fiona.' Falcon wasn't prepared to compromise, and Loxley realized that.

'No problem.' Loxley conceded. 'For the moment at least, we seem to be in agreement. Fiona stays the core priority in the investigation. But if hard evidence proving the existence of the killer turns up, we switch direction. We can't sit back if a serial killer appears in the mix.'

It was the first head to head clash, and confrontation had been avoided. But Fiona got the impression that the two officers were sparring with each other, trying to establish which one should assume the mantle of the alpha male. But of course it was a totally unequal contest, she thought. For one very simple reason. Rank. She sensed that Loxley seemed reluctant to play that card – so far, at least – and Fiona wondered what would happen if a full blown disagreement blew up.

'So turning to the core investigation,' Loxley said. 'We have two possible names in the frame for the assault on Fiona. Debbie Connelly and Adam Devine. Apparently, they both believe they have good grounds to hate Fiona for what she's done to their lives. Certain aspects of the case have all the hallmarks of Debbie Connelly, and her need to be centre stage, written all over them. But at the moment, Adam Devine is just a name, and we can't prove that there's even any kind of connection between him and Debbie Connelly. So, as of now, they're simply two individuals who might have a grievance against Fiona.'

Just then Goldilocks came into the room. 'Sorry I'm late, but we've had problems in the computer centre.'

'Adam Levine.' Loxley came straight to the point. 'Do you have any more information on him, Sergeant?'

'Sorry, but as soon as we started checking the various databases with our latest software package the system crashed. It's a new programme and the techies are working on it. But at the moment I'm afraid I don't have anything else on Adam Devine.'

'When will the system be online again?' Falcon asked.

'Best estimate's some time tomorrow morning,' Goldilocks replied.

'OK.' Falcon came in. 'Right now, we can't connect Adam

ROY CHESTER

Devine and Debbie Connelly. For one thing, we simply don't know
enough about Devine, and we won't until the computer system's
running again. But I have a question for Fiona. You were responsible for Adam Levine losing his liberty for a few years. I accept
that. But would it be a sufficient motive for him to come after you
just to exert vengeance?'

'Vengeance can be a very strong motive,' Fiona replied. 'And I
wouldn't be surprised if Adam Levine held a grudge that festered
with time.'

'I agree,' Carl Lucas said. 'With some individuals, a grudge can
lead to a sense of deep-seated hurt that goes on building up until
it's released.'

'And how would it be released?' Loxley asked.

'By fulfilling the act of vengeance.'

Falcon looked at him. Lucas had obviously decided that he was
going to be pro-active and not simply an observer at the briefings.
But for the moment Falcon let it go.

'Fiona?' Loxley came back to her.

'Carl's right,' Fiona said. 'The effects holding a grudge will have
on some individuals can be very strong. In some cases it could
actually become an obsession. So let's see what we have on Debbie
Connelly and Adam Devine.'

Fiona walked over to a whiteboard clipped to the wall behind
the table and picked up a marker pen. Then she started to write on
the board.

Debbie Connelly – data from previous investigation.
    Low self-esteem
    Actress
    Attention seeker
    Manipulative
    Vicious when thwarted

*Adam Devine – data mainly from the assessment carried out at
Warings Hospital.*
    Loner

Computer nerd
Bi-polar
Vicious when under the influence of alcohol

Common Factor

Both hold a grudge against me because they believe I'm
responsible for locking them away.

Motive

Revenge

Opportunity

Debbie Connelly conned her way out of the clinic where
she was being held and committed suicide – fake?
Adam Devine – no info at this stage

'Interesting characters.' Carl Lucas read the material on the
board. 'Particularly Debbie Connelly. Manipulative and vicious
when thwarted. As evidenced in the past by trapping Fiona in the
glass lift with the aim of killing her. And now you suspect that she
faked her own suicide?'

'But that's all it is.' Falcon replied. 'A suspicion.'

Loxley nodded. 'True. But at this stage we have enough to tag
Debbie Connelly as a prime suspect, at least until we learn
anything to the contrary. Adam Levine, we leave on hold. But
Fiona's already supplied a photograph of Debbie Connelly, and I
suggest we get one of Adam Devine in case it's needed later.'

'I'll get on to the clinic in Cornwall,' Goldilocks said, leaving the
room.

'Back to the letter, do you think Debbie Connelly could have
written it?' Lucas asked.

'We don't even know it was written by a woman,' Fiona said.
'But let's take another look.'

Falcon walked over to the far wall and extracted a red file from
a numbered evidence box. Placing it down on the table, he opened
it and handed the letter to Fiona. She read it a few times, then
handed it back to Falcon.

'Difficult to be certain, but if I had to make a judgement I'd say the letter was written by a woman.'

'Can I see it again, please?' Carl Lucas held out his hand.

Falcon gave him the letter, which he read.

'It could have been written by a woman, I agree. But it would take an expert to prove it.'

'Leaving that aside for now, what about the rest of the letter?' Loxley said. 'Specifically, the threats made to Fiona?'

Falcon read the last paragraph of the letter aloud:

'*Next, she* [Fiona] *will step outside the pale and become the subject of a major police search. But it could be too late for Fiona as the evidence against her begins to stack up. Evidence that will lead you to the serial killer and shock you to the core. Poor little Fiona.*'

'I don't like this.' Loxley sounded worried.

'I'm not exactly over the moon about it myself,' Fiona snapped back. 'The implication that I'll step outside the pale and then lead you to a serial killer. It's all riddles. Far-fetched nonsense. Except, that kind of nonsense is par for the course for Debbie Connelly. It's exactly the kind of theatre she goes for.'

'So we take it very seriously,' Loxley said. 'And we keep you safe. For tonight you stay in your apartment, and I'll put a couple of officers there to watch the place. Then we'll review the situation tomorrow and see if we need to up the level of security.'

'I'll stay with Fiona,' Goldilocks said. 'Just for reassurance.'

'Thanks, I'd appreciate that,' Fiona replied.

'In the meantime, we'll get Carl fixed up with a hotel.'

'What about dinner?' Carl Lucas asked Fiona. 'Would you and Sergeant Maltravers like to join me?'

'Sorry,' Fiona said. 'But I think Superintendent Loxley would like to keep me under some kind of curfew in my apartment tonight.'

Just as the meeting was about to break up, one of Goldilocks's team came in with a computer printout.

'The system came back online quicker than we expected and here's the data on Adam Devine you asked for.'

She handed the print-out to Goldilocks, who read through the data quickly.

'Got it.' She turned to Loxley. 'The connection between Debbie Connelly and Adam Devine. They were both patients at the same mental health clinic in Cornwall. And apparently, they formed a relationship while they were there. Adam Devine was the unknown friend who was close to Debbie Connelly.'

'So he can join Debbie Connelly in the frame as a prime suspect.'

'But even though we put them in the frame, we still don't have any proof that either of them are actually involved in the case, do we?' Falcon brought them back to earth.

Loxley shook his head. 'As of yet, no. We don't have any proof.'

The briefing broke up then, but as Lucas was leaving the office Falcon called him back.

'The letter.'

'Yes.'

'The tiny matter of the serial killer. Either the information in the letter sent to you is wrong, or we have a real live serial killer on the streets of Garton.'

'You sound sceptical, Detective Chief Inspector.'

'Oh, I'm sceptical all right. What was it the letter said? *One of the most terrible serial killers this country has ever seen.*' So how come there's been no trace of this killer? Not even a whisper.'

13

She flew across the carpet and hurled herself into his arms, a small bundle of warmth.

'Princess.' Falcon held her tightly, breathing in the bath fresh smell as her arms went around his neck.

She twisted her head free and looked at him, her eyes solemn. 'You said you'd be home early today, Daddy.'

'I know, Princess. And I'm sorry, but I came as soon as I could.'

'Simon couldn't keep awake. He tried, but he fell asleep and Mummy took him to bed.'

'And you'll have to go now, young lady.' Denise Falcon ruffled the girl's hair.

'But Daddy's only just got here.' Susan turned to her mother, her voice plaintive and cajoling. But suddenly she gave a huge yawn. 'I am a *bit* tired,' she admitted reluctantly. 'But I can stay awake long enough for a story.'

'All right, go on then, but just one chapter.' She smiled at Falcon. 'Dinner will be about an hour.'

'You heard what Mummy said. One chapter. Then I can grab a shower.' He marched away, swinging the little girl from side to side.

When he came into the kitchen later he was wearing a track suit and trainers, and he groaned as he slid onto a tall chair at the breakfast bar.

'Here.' She handed him a tall glass with ice and a slice of lemon floating on the surface. 'Gin and tonic. Just as Sir likes it.'

'Thanks.' He lifted it to his lips, savouring the sharp clean taste. 'I'm sorry. I know I said I'd be home early, but something came up.'

She put down the bowl she was using to toss a salad and moved across the floor to stand in front of him.

'It's all right, lover. I understand the pressure you're under. Really, I do. And remember, you told me this investigation is to protect Fiona from someone trying to harm her. And Fiona's a friend. More than that, she's Simon's godmother. So, are you any closer to an arrest?'

'Let's just say, things are moving.'

'And what about working with the new super?'

'As usual, you cut to the chase.'

'And?'

Falcon realized she wasn't going to be put off. 'You remember what they called me when I first joined the service?'

'The "golden boy".'

'That's right. The "golden boy". A university law graduate on the fast track promotion. And to put the icing on the cake, a black man. The perfect recipe for a truly distinguished career in this modern politically conscious police service. Except for one thing.'

'Your Dad.'

'That's right. My Daddy. Jeremiah Falcon.'

Jeremiah Falcon. The most prominent lawyer in the city, at least among the criminal fraternity. 'Villain's Friend' and 'Scourge of the Police' were among the names he'd been called at various times by the media. And in addition to his law work, Jeremiah Falcon was a nationally famous black activist and had served on the recent government commission on 'Racial Equality in the Workplace'. He'd been involved in bringing to light a racial scandal within the Garton police force – a scandal that had resulted in the resignation of the chief constable. But it had made no friends for his son on the force.

'But surely nothing your father does can affect your career?'

Falcon shrugged. 'Perhaps not on the surface. Underneath, who knows what stones are waiting to be turned? There's more than one officer at police HQ that my dad's crossed, mostly in court. But worst of all was the part he played in bringing down the chief constable for the racial comments he'd made. Guilt by association.

You know how it works. And don't forget, they brought in an outsider to do ACC Malloy's old job.'

'So what about working under this guy Loxley?'

'I wanted the promotion, true. And I can't argue that I felt let down when I didn't get it. But as to whether I can work under Loxley, only time will tell.'

'But surely, other chances of promotion will come up, won't they? Or is there something else. Something you haven't told me about?'

'Maybe.'

She grabbed his wrist and twisted it. 'Tell. Tell!'

'OK, you've got me banged to rights, officer.'

Falcon gently drew her towards him, holding her close. Then he held her away and looked at her. Denise Falcon was a beauty. 'Tall and slim with legs that seem to stretch forever, and the face of a mischievous angel', was how one fashion writer had described her when she'd first burst onto the modelling scene. Now, ten years and two children later, she had lost none of that beauty. If anything, she had acquired a mature serenity that enhanced her looks, giving her a softness that hadn't been there before.

'Did I ever tell you how good it is to be able to come home and find you there?'

'A few times. And I'm always ready to hear it again. But don't think for one second, Gary Falcon, that you can side-track me like this. So tell me what's worrying you?'

'It's Dad. He's been on to me several times to jack in the police and join the law firm.'

'So what's new?'

'What's knew is that I think he's worried about something. Very worried.'

'Like he's ill, you mean?'

'I don't know. So far, he clams up every time I mention the subject. But he's asked me to meet him this evening in a pretty remote location.'

'All a bit cloak and dagger, isn't it?'

'Exactly.'

'And you're going there?'

'Yes, I have to.'

'You do that. But just be careful. And by the way, I'm seeing your mother tomorrow, so maybe I can draw her out a bit?'

'If there is a problem I'm not sure he would have confided in her. He's a very private man. But I guess it's worth a try. Why are you going to see my mother? Any special reason?'

'There might be. Just might be.'

'So now it's your turn. Tell.'

'Or what, big man?'

'I might just have to put you over my knee before arresting you for withholding information.'

'Now that's a thought. But seriously, you remember Shirley Crompton?'

'Your ex-agent?'

'That's right. Well, she was on the phone today to offer me some work. One of the big stores is promoting a new line for the middle thirties woman. Mature but glamorous. And they actually asked for me to front the campaign. Just think of it, little me. Even though I'm old and decrepit now. All the shooting will be here in the North West so I won't have to spend nights away, but we'll need someone to look after the kids during the day. Take them to nursery, collect them. Just be there for them. I'm sure your mother would love to do it. '

'I'm sure she would. And we could do with the money. The way you and those twins there spend it these days.'

He tried to move aside as she jabbed at his ribs with her elbow, only partially succeeding.

'OK, OK. It's a great idea.' He grinned. 'Oh, and by the way, I don't agree with the bit about you being old. Decrepit, maybe. But you're only as old as I am.'

This time he caught the full force of her elbow.

14

Falcon pulled the car off the road and onto the car park in the shadow of the large brick buildings of an old power station. The station had been decommissioned two years ago, and was to be incorporated in a riverside development which would include up-market apartments, a shopping mall and a marina. But for now, the place was deserted, and weeds were growing through cracks in the tarmac surface.

A vehicle was drawn up on the far side of the car park and, as he approached, Falcon recognized his father's Mercedes. He parked alongside it, switched off his engine, and got out of the car. There was a hint of damp drizzle on the air as he walked round to the Mercedes. The window on the driver's side was down and cigar smoke drifted out.

'Thank you for coming, Gary.' But there was no smile of greeting, and for a moment Falcon thought his father wasn't even going to get out of the car. Then, finally, he opened the door and stood on the tarmac.

Typical of the way their relationship had deteriorated, Falcon thought.

At that moment, a large lorry moved along the dock road and Falcon caught a glimpse of his father's face in the headlights. He was shocked. His father looked to have aged ten years since the last time he'd seen him at the twin's birthday party a few weeks ago. The skin on his face seemed to hang slack now, and Falcon wondered if Denise had been right after all and his father was ill.

The two figures stood there in the shadow of the power station – close together, but a hundred miles apart.

How had it come to this, Falcon wondered? To a stage where they had difficulty even speaking to each other? Falcon knew things had got worse after the twin's party when he'd finally rejected his father's entreaties to leave the police and join the family law firm.

They were in the garden with time to talk as Denise and Falcon's mother put the twins to bed. And Falcon could remember every word of the conversation.

'Be a lawyer, Gary. It's what you were trained for before you joined the force. And remember, I'm not getting any younger.'

'I'm happy enough being with the police.'

'But are you? I understand there are big changes afoot in Crime Management. How much of that will you be a part of?'

Falcon felt shock touch him. He should have realized his father had contacts deep inside the force.

'You've heard something?' Falcon had tried to keep his voice neutral.

'I'm always hearing *something*. The Garton Police Service leaks like a sieve.'

'And on this particular issue of the reorganization?'

'I understand that power struggles are in the offing, and that you didn't get the promotion you were hoping for.'

'I know about the power struggles from my own source in the hierarchy.'

'You have your own source? Now that surprises me. I never had you down as enough of a political animal for that.'

Even though he realized it was petty, Falcon felt he'd scored a point there.

'True, I'll never be a bruiser like you. But even a leopard can change its spots.'

'And what about ambition? Or, in your case, maybe a lack of it.'

'Is that how you see me? No ambition?'

'Not without any ambition, no. More a lack of the *kind* of ambition that a senior officer in the police must have. And with missing out on your promotion, maybe this could be the perfect time for a career change.'

But Falcon had stood his ground, and told his father he was staying with the police. He didn't say that one reason for not joining the law firm was that he didn't think he could work with his father looking over his shoulder all the time and picking endless faults. He'd kept it to himself, but after that talk things between them had gone even further downhill. And yet it was his father who had asked for this meeting.

Something was wrong, Falcon could sense it.

'I came here because you asked me to. So?' It came out with more aggression than Falcon intended.

'We've got problems, Gary.' His father's voice was a low whisper, and Falcon had to lean forward to catch the words.

'What kind of problems?'

'Problems to do with the Lewis drug smuggling trial.'

'You're representing one of the defendants, right?'

'Yes. But my client has invoked the Serious Organised Crime and Police Act, and decided to offer Queen's evidence and testify against Eric Lewis, the gang boss. He took that line on my advice on the strict understanding that he would go into the witness protection programme, and be provided with immunity. So he's hidden away, out of Lewis's reach. And, apart from his police handlers, there's only one person who can get to him.'

'His lawyer.'

'Yes, his lawyer. Lewis knows that. And he's threatened violence unless I persuade my client to retract his statement.'

Falcon was surprised. His father wasn't normally intimidated by threats against him.

'You've dealt with this kind of thing before, haven't you?'

The older man ground his cigar out on the tarmac and turned to Falcon, fear evident in his eyes now.

'Yes, I've faced intimidation in the past. But this is different. This time the threats aren't against me.'

Falcon felt a stab of unease. 'So who are they against?'

'Denise and the twins.'

'Jesus.' Falcon suddenly felt the weight of the world press down on him.

'Lewis gave me a deadline. Persuade my client to withdraw his offer to turn Queen's evidence by this weekend, or he comes after the family. So get them somewhere safe, Gary. And do it now. Don't wait for the deadline to run out.'

Falcon nodded, forcing himself to act logically. Then he went back to his car and phoned Loxley using his mobile. Once he'd contacted the superintendent, Falcon requested an immediate watch be put on his house, saying he would explain when he arrived at Police HQ. Then he phoned Denise and breathed a sigh of relief when he found she was still at the house with the kids. He told her not be alarmed if she saw a police car outside, and that he'd explain later. But until he arrived no one was to leave the house. Then he drove straight back to HQ, where Loxley was waiting in his office.

'What's happening, Gary? Have we got problems?'

'It's not our case. It's the Lewis drug investigation.'

He went on to explain about his father, and Lewis's threats against Denise and the kids.

When he'd finished Loxley nodded. 'Your order of priorities was spot on. Safety of your family comes first. So what sort of character is this Lewis?'

'He's a nasty, vicious little sod.'

'Then I think we should move your family to a safe house soonest, and keep them there under guard. How will your wife react to that?'

'As long as the safety of the kids is involved she'll co-operate fully.'

'Good. I'll put the arrangements in place. You go to your present address and put your wife in the picture. Then we'll transfer the family to a safe house using a secure route and hold them there. But from now you have no face to face contact with them. You know as well as I do how important security is in this kind of oper-ation. Right?'

'Right.'

'Good. And when your family's safe, I'll put the head of the Lewis team in the picture.'

Falcon was impressed at the way Loxley had handled the situation. Maybe he'd misjudged him, Falcon thought as he left to explain the situation to Denise.

Or maybe in the cosmic scheme of things there were more important issues than a potential vendetta between two police officers.

15

The noise was insistent. Drilling into her mind.

Fire alarm.

Fiona recognized the noise, and she automatically threw back the duvet and swung her legs onto the floor. Without thinking she looked at the alarm clock on a table by the side of her bed. The red digital figures showed 1.50. Then Goldilocks came into the bedroom pulling on a pair of jeans.

'Fire alarm. Get dressed. We have to get out of here.' She tossed Fiona the clothes that were lying on a chair under the window, and as she dressed Goldilocks used her mobile to contact the police watching the building from outside on the street.

She told the officer who took the call to bring his partner inside and wait by the door of the apartment. But already tendrils of dark smoke were seeping into the flat, and they could hear voices outside in the corridor. Then suddenly the front door burst open and two figures – a woman wearing a cape and a man dressed in a heavy overcoat – thrust themselves inside, shouting something about people being trapped in the flat. Both of them wore scarves wrapped around their faces to protect them from smoke inhalation.

As the door splintered the burglar alarm went off, adding another level of noise to the chaos. Ignoring the alarm, the two figures pushed Fiona and Goldilocks back inside the apartment, pulled the remains of the front door shut, and dragged them into separate rooms.

Everything had happened so quickly and Fiona was still disorientated when the figure holding her suddenly forced her lips apart and poured liquid from a plastic bottle down her throat. Fiona coughed, but the woman held her tight.

While that was happening the man bound Goldilocks with duct tape, then stabbed a needle into her arm. When her body went slack, he pushed her out of sight under the bed.

'Stay behind and try and set up a diversion. I'll see you later at the hut.' Fiona heard the words but she seemed curiously detached, as if everything was happening to someone else.

'Stay close.' The woman led Fiona outside. In the corridor it was chaos. A mass of people were milling around and shouting in the thick oily smoke that reduced visibility to a few yards. In the confusion, no one took any notice of one woman leading another to safety. Following behind, the man let them reach the end of the corridor, then started to scream about the danger from a gas escape. The warning set off a wave of panic as the people still in the corridor twisted and turned, surging one way and then another in a mad rush. The police officers were swept along with the tide, and when they did regain some control of the situation they concentrated on getting the people away from the fictitious gas leak.

It was cold in the thin wind that came in off the river, and Fiona was glad of the anorak and boots she'd put on at Goldilocks insistence. But something was wrong. She was walking away, going further and further from her apartment. For a moment she wondered what had happened to Goldilocks. But even that question drifted away again.

They skirted the car park at the rear of the apartment block, and when they reached the main dock road they crossed and entered the financial area of the city on the other side. At one stage, Fiona thought she heard the siren of a fire engine, but she couldn't be certain, and anyway she didn't really care as she became more and more confused.

In a strange kind of way, Fiona knew she should go back. But she could no more do that than change night into day. She didn't know why, but she was being drawn into something. She had no idea what, but she was helpless to fight against it. And that stirred up a feeling of terror. Of something waiting for her in the night.

The buildings stretched upwards towards the sky. Old, ornately-styled insurance and banking houses. Memorials to Garton's past as a great port. Occasionally, edifices of concrete and glass thrust into the skyline, confident symbols of the regeneration of the city.

The streetlights were scarce, and the dark alleyways between the buildings were sinister spaces inhabited by shadows. Fiona could imagine creatures in there, waiting to attack the interlopers. And still she was drawn deeper and deeper into the surrealistic landscape.

Then the figure turned and moved onto a steep street leading down to an area of old derelict dock buildings. A ghostly moon came out of the clouds, turning the surface of the river into quick-silver and softening the outlines of the buildings with a pale wash. And there was a mist on the air, drifting across the open spaces. They moved deeper into the shadow world of skeletal structures, and Fiona continued to let the woman lead her because it meant she didn't have to think for herself. They crossed several patches of open ground, stumbling over the rough surface. All the time the smell of the river hung on the air, mixed with the pungent smoke from a fire.

Then Fiona saw them. Figures sitting around an oil drum with a fire inside it. There must have been ten or twelve people there, some holding bottles. But despite the hour, few of them seemed to be sleeping. They were dressed in vagrant clothing – old raincoats, ex-army greatcoats, dirt-stained reefer jackets and, incongruously, one man was wearing what looked like a full dinner suit.

Most of the vagrants were locked away in their own worlds and showed no interest in the strangers. But one of them, a girl in her late teens, looked up as they approached. 'Hey. Got anything to drink?'

'Here.' The woman leading Fiona pulled a bottle wrapped in brown paper from the pocket in her cape. 'All for you. If you're a good girl.'

The girl tried to snatch the bottle, but the woman stood back.

'What do you want me to do?' There was a pathetic eagerness in the words now.

'It's simple really. I need to take my friend here to another place. But she's very tired and she needs support. So if you'll help us, the bottle will be yours when we come back. Deal?'

'Deal.' The girl put her arm around Fiona's shoulder and led her away, following the woman in the cape.

16

'Sorry to call you back in, Gary, but all hell's broken loose since you left to take care of your family. Are they settled in the safe house, by the way?'

'No problem. The kids think it's a big adventure, and Denise is just glad they're safe. So what's been going down here?'

'First, in the light of what's happened vis à vis your family, do you want to be taken off this case to be with them.'

'No.' Falcon shook his head emphatically. 'As long as they're safe I'd rather stay on here.'

'Good.' Loxley smiled, seeming genuinely pleased. 'To begin with, I didn't contact you until your family were completely settled at the safe house. My decision. I knew it would be a stressful time uprooting them, and I didn't want any extra pressure put on you.'

'Thanks, I appreciate that.'

As Loxley walked over to a white board that he'd been using, Falcon noticed that two large coloured photographs, one of Debbie Connelly and the other of Adam Devine, had been attached to a glass display panel.

Loxley stood in front of the white board.

'As you can see I've tried to put the night's events into some kind of order. At one fifty five a 999 call reported a fire at a block of flats by the docks. When the emergency services arrived the situation there was very confused, but as they were clearing the building the fire fighters found a woman bound and gagged in one of the apartments. It was Sergeant Maltravers, who'd been staying with Fiona. Once she'd been freed the sergeant used her mobile to

raise the officers who'd been on surveillance outside the apartment. It turned out that they'd already tried to contact her, but she
couldn't respond because she was bound and gagged at the time.
The officers had come into the building to protect Fiona, but in all
the chaos they couldn't locate her. At that stage, Sergeant
Maltravers was found by the fire fighters and she reported to HQ.
It was then that I was informed '

'And Fiona?'

'She disappeared into thin air. In all the confusion on the
corridor, no one seems to have seen a woman fitting Fiona's
description.'

'So we can assume she'd been abducted?' Falcon said.

'At the time it looked that way. Then another incident was
reported. At 4.35 a call came in to Police HQ, with a warning that
Fiona Nightingale was in one of the areas where the vagrants meet
by the docks. The caller was a female and she broke the connection
after delivering the message. It turns out she was using an
untraceable 'pay-as-you-go' mobile. Anyway, the duty inspector
dispatched a patrol car to the scene where they found Fiona
among the vagrants. As promised.'

'Where is she now?'

'In Garton General. Apparently she'd been drugged. They're
keeping her in for the rest of the night, but the doctors reckon
she'll be ready for discharge around noon tomorrow. Or today, in
fact.'

'Shit.' Loxley shook his head. 'First, the incident at the fountain,
then the fire hoax at the apartment, and now she turns up with the
down-and-outs. Our Fiona's putting herself about a bit isn't she?'

'It certainly looks that way.' Falcon had to agree.

'You worried?' Loxley picked up something in Falcon's voice.

Falcon shrugged. 'Despite what Fiona says herself, I don't think
she's recovered from the incident in the glass lift yet. She's still
fragile, and any more stress might just tip her over the edge.'

17

Loxley and Falcon escorted Fiona to her flat when she was discharged from hospital the following afternoon. There was still a remnant smell of smoke from the last evening, but the shattered front door had been repaired by the company that had the maintenance contract on the building.

'Look, if you'd rather put this off until tomorrow morning that's not a problem,' Loxley said, worried by Fiona's haggard appearance.

'No, it's OK. I know I have to answer some questions, and it's good of you to come here.'

They sat down around a small glass topped table, by the window overlooking the estuary.

Loxley turned to Fiona. 'This isn't a formal interview, but we might need to make it official later. The way it looks now, at least three crimes have been committed. First, the arson attack on your apartment block. Second, your abduction. And third, the illegal administration of drugs to you. But at the moment we just want to establish what happened last night.'

'I understand,' she said, sounding tired.

'OK.' Loxley seemed relieved. 'I'm going to let Gary lead because he knows you better than I do.'

'I understand from the doctors that you were drugged,' Falcon began.

'Yes. It was administered from a plastic water bottle.'

'What drug was it?'

'According to the tox screen they ran, it was Rohypnol.'

'The date rape drug?' Loxley came in.

'Yes. But I wasn't raped. I know that because as soon as they told me I'd been given Rohypnol, I asked for an internal examination.'

'Was it the same drug used on you in the incident at the glass fountain?' Falcon asked.

Fiona shrugged. 'I don't know because the original sample for a tox screen appears to have gone missing.'

'So why use that particular drug on you this time?' Falcon asked.

'I think it must have been because it would reduce my resistance, and cause some degree of amnesia.'

'So that you wouldn't remember what happened to you?'

'Yes, so I wouldn't remember,' Fiona said. 'But I've no idea why that should be important to whoever took me?'

'That's what we need to find out,' Falcon said. 'So if you can take us through what you do remember it might help. From the beginning, please.'

Fiona shrugged. A small hopeless gesture, and for a moment Falcon thought she was going to break down.

'That's the problem, Gary. Because of the drug there *was* no beginning. I have a vague recollection of wandering down deserted city streets being led by someone. Then I was down at the docks, in the mist, with people sat around a fire in an oil drum.'

'So let's concentrate on the person who was leading you,' Falcon said. 'Can you remember anything about them? Anything at all?'

'Only odd impressions, nothing else. But I'm certain it was a woman, and to begin with she was wearing a heavy coat. But she gave it to me later, and she was wearing a buff coloured anorak underneath.'

'And her face?' Falcon asked.

Fiona shook her head. 'She kept the scarf in place all the time.'

'So.' Falcon smiled. 'You can remember some things. Let's take a look at the time you spent down at the docks with the vagrants. What happened when you first got there?'

Fiona tried to concentrate.

'All that walking in the dark streets had tired me out. I remember that. I just wanted to lie down and rest. But the woman wouldn't let me. She said we had to go somewhere else.'

'Where was this other place?' Falcon asked.

Fiona felt the panic rising. 'I don't remember.' She stood up and started to walk away.

Falcon caught her arm and gently drew her back. 'It's OK. You're doing fine. Don't forget, you've been drugged.'

'It's just so bloody frustrating. Everything's on the edge of my mind, but I can't draw it in.'

'I think maybe we should leave this until your mind's back on track,' Falcon said.

'No, wait a moment. Something's there. We didn't stay by the oil drum for long. I remember that because one of the vagrants, a young woman, helped me to walk away. I don't know where we went, or what we did, but I can remember coming back to the docks later and joining the rest of the crowd round the fire in the oil drum. I can also remember that the girl who'd led me away wasn't with us any longer. And come to that, neither was the woman that had taken me to the vagrants in the first place. But I was cold then because I wasn't wearing her coat.'

'Can we put up any kind of a time line here?' Falcon asked.

Fiona shook her head. 'Sorry, but I've no idea how long we'd been away.'

'OK.' Falcon didn't want to rush things. 'Let's see if we can narrow it down a bit. What time did you go to bed?' he asked Fiona.

'About half past eleven, quarter to twelve. But I can do better than that. When the fire alarm woke me up it was 1.50 on my bedside clock.' She sounded pleased that she'd remembered that.

'It's a mile or so from your apartment to where the vagrants meet. Say a twenty minute walk, thirty perhaps if you were drugged and tiring. So you'd get there around 2.20. You don't think you stayed long, but the police weren't contacted and told you were there until 4.35. So, at a rough estimate you were gone from the place where the vagrants were for around two hours. Can you remember anything about those two hours? Anything at all?'

'No, sorry. Nothing. It's a total blank canvas.' She yawned suddenly.

'I think that's about enough for now,' Falcon said. 'After last night's fiasco we've upped the security on you. We've stationed an officer outside your door, and there's a patrol car by the entrance to the apartment block. You'll be safe. Unless you want to go somewhere else?'

'No, I'll be all right here. I just want to go to sleep for a few hours.'

'Good idea. What's your schedule for today?'

'I don't have anything at the hospital until half past eleven. So I can get a few hours' sleep.'

'I'll arrange transport for you to and from the hospital.'

As they came out of the building, Loxley turned to Falcon.

'What happened in those missing two hours, Gary? That could be the key to all this.'

'Maybe you're right,' Falcon said. 'But nothing's really clear yet.'

18

The car bringing Fiona from the hospital dropped her at the apartment block, and the driver handed her over to a waiting officer who escorted her upstairs. He must have been given strict instructions on Fiona's safety because when they were upstairs he took the key to the apartment from her and opened the door. When she'd disabled the alarm the officer told her to wait while he checked the apartment. When he'd done that he stayed outside in the corridor.

It had been a long day, and all Fiona wanted was a shower. But as she entered the living room she received a call from the security desk. The operator told her a package had been delivered to the desk for her collection.

She told the officer outside in the corridor, and he went to collect it. After he verified that there was nothing in the envelope except a DVD in a plastic case he gave it to Fiona. She was back in the living room when her mobile rang. She removed it from her handbag and took the call.

'You'd better watch the DVD now, lady. Because we're having it shown on the six forty five news slot on Vista TV. And believe me, you really don't want to be around when it goes out.'

The caller was a woman, but she'd ended the call before Fiona could reply. Fiona put the phone away, turned on the TV set and placed the DVD in the disc player. Before it started to run the phone rang again.

For a moment there was silence on the other end of the line. Then the voice. Muffled and throaty. The same woman.

'We've been a naughty girl, haven't we, Fiona?'

'Who is this?'

'Murderer.'

The word was screeched, the voice high pitched now.

'Play the disc. And leave the mobile open.'

It was only then that Fiona realized her hands was shaking. She forced herself to stay calm and set the DVD player to play. As she watched, a grainy black and white image appeared on the screen. At first, Fiona thought the TV set was still warming-up, but when she recognized the stretch of waterfront with the ferry terminal in the background, she realized she was watching CCTV footage.

The data at the bottom of the picture indicated that the sequence had started at 3.06 a.m. the previous night. The numbers continued to change as the film showed a deserted area by the side of the ferry booking office. Then at 3.10 a.m. two figures came into view, both women. They appeared to be fighting, and one of them had the other by the hair. As they continued to struggle the woman gripping her opponent's hair lifted a piece of what looked like rubble from a pocket and smashed it several times against the other woman's head. Then she paused and checked her for vital signs. She mustn't have found any because she tossed the stone into the waters of the dock and rolled the body after it. As she did so she was caught by the camera as she turned away.

And Fiona gasped.

It was her face. She was the person wielding the stone. The features of the killer were her features.

Then the voice came over the mobile.

'Murderer. You remember now, don't you? Now that you've seen it. Did it feel good? Such power. And all in your hands. But you'd better run, Fiona. Run, run, run. Because Vesta TV will show the sequence this evening and the police will come after you. With all the stops out. Is anywhere safe for you now? Anywhere at all? There is one place, yes. Try the Waste Land. The vagrants will show you the way, and when you're there you'll be amongst old friends. And then you'll know the final answer.'

Fiona knew she hadn't killed that woman – except she'd just seen herself carry out the murder on TV. And soon, so would millions of viewers.

So how had they made her do it? Drugs? In her profession, she knew well enough the power of drugs. Had she been fed one of the strong hallucinatory drugs? She didn't know. But one thing stuck out. The murder had been committed sometime during the missing two hours.

And she had to get to the Waste Land to learn the truth.

19

In her present state of mind Fiona recognized only one reality. She had to get away. But as the voice on the phone had asked, was anywhere safe? Then the question had been answered for her. The Waste Land was safe.

She stood at the door of the apartment wracked by indecision. When the CCTV disc was released she would be branded a murderer. She would be outside the pale then. No friends, and the full might of the law against her.

Then she remembered the down-and-outs by the riverside, and fuzzy snatches of memory surfaced at the edges of her mind.

Why had she had been taken there? She had no idea. But there must have been a reason, and for the moment she focused on that.

The voice on the phone had told her to go to the vagrants who would show her into the Waste Land. So maybe the answer lay with them. In any case, she had nobody else to turn to. She had to get to the vagrants – to take the one chance she'd get of learning the truth.

She glanced at her watch. She still had a few minutes before the TV programme started.

'Damn.' She swore under her breath. The officer outside. He wouldn't know about the item that was coming up on TV, but he wouldn't let her go anywhere on her own either. And as soon the programme went out the first thing the police would do was to contact the officer over the radio net and get him to detain her. She moved out into the hall and slipped on a heavy anorak she took from the hook near the door, and picked up her handbag. Then she opened the door. The officer was sitting on a chair positioned opposite the apartment, and he started to stand up as saw the door open.

Fiona rushed across the corridor and pushed him as he was half way out of the chair. He fell to the floor and Fiona ran to the stairs. As soon as she reached the emergency exit she opened the bar release and stepped out onto the fire escape. When she came to the ground she ran under a stone arch and stood to the side, hidden in the shadows as she faced the quayside. As the officer came round the corner she stepped out from behind the arch and crashed her shoulder into his chest. Caught completely off guard he spun away and fell into the water of the dock.

Muttering an apology, Fiona carried on across the open space, following the route she'd been taken the previous night as far as she could remember it. Behind her, a figure wearing a long dark coat and hood stayed in the shadows, watching. Then she moved out, following Fiona.

As she turned out onto the main dock road Fiona heard the sirens and saw the blue flashing lights of the approaching police cars. She kept to the shadows as she moved through the financial district, and as she approached the derelict dock area she saw the down-and-outs on the edge of the shore sitting around the oil drum. Just like the last time she'd come here.

It was a place of shadows and Fiona moved forward across a surface of compacted clay, stumbling over the bricks and lengths of old timber scattered across the ground. The smell of the river, dank with slime, carried from the black stretch of water dimly visible between the shells of the tall warehouses looming through the murk. And something else was on the air – a mixture of foetid bodies and oily smoke.

Figures were clustered around a fire burning in the oil drum, shapes that moved in the dancing flames. They were dressed in an odd mixture of old clothes and some held bottles in their hands. But they all seemed indifferent to the intruder, as if they inhabited another world – which Fiona supposed they did.

She was panting, and she doubled over to get her breath back. Then she approached the circle sitting around the oil drum on old car seats.

'Do any of you remember me? I was here last night. A woman brought me.'

Only the crackling of the wood broke the silence.

'Please, you have to help me.'

Still nothing but silence from the figures around the oil drum.

'I can pay.' She took her purse out of a pocket in her anorak and extracted a twenty pound note.

That stirred the vagrants, and one of them stood up. He was wearing an old army greatcoat and a bowler hat. He stood in front of Fiona and held out his hand. She backed away, and he muttered something under his breath and tried to snatch the note. But he stumbled and fell over. He lay there on the ground, his breath coming in odd rasping sounds. Then he forced himself to his knees.

'The woman who brought you here. We'd never seen her before. None of us. She wasn't a regular.'

Fiona felt the hope drain away. 'But she brought me here, yes?'

'Yes, she brought you here.'

'But what did she do with me them?'

'She asked Glenda to help her take you somewhere. Promised her a bottle if she did so.'

And what happened?' Fiona felt her hopes rise again.

'They dragged you away, the two of them. But I know where they took you?'

'Where?'

The man forced himself to his feet and held out his hand. 'Money first.'

Fiona realized that if she handed over the note he could simply walk away with it. But she had no choice really so she handed him the money.

'Now tell me.' She tried to put some authority in her voice. 'Where did they take me?'

'Away over there.' He pointed to the north. And I heard the woman say something about going to the ferry terminal. Then they took you away, and when you came back Glenda wasn't with you any longer.'

'What happened then?' Fiona was beginning to feel that they were getting close to the truth now.

'The woman left you here with us. Then she went away.'

'Do you know where to?'

'Oh, I know where she went, all right. But it won't do you any good. You can't follow her. Not where she's gone.'

He laughed.

'And where's that?'

'In there.' He pointed down river.

'But why should that be a problem?'

'Because it's a way into the Waste Land. And there are things in there. Things you don't want to know about.'

And still the figure waited in the shadows.

20

Fiona hesitated. She knew this was a turning point. Ahead of her she could see a long stretch of chain link fence with a gap in it. On the other side of that fence there was nothing to protect her.

Why was she being driven towards the Waste Land? Was she walking straight into a trap?

But she had to know where they'd taken her to the previous night, and before she had time to change her mind, she crossed a thin strip of black mud and stopped in front of the chain link fence that cut off the Waste Land. But someone had wrenched out the last section of fence and at low tide it was possible to walk through onto the other side.

Into the Waste Land.

Gingerly, avoiding the sharp edges of metal, she slipped through the gap into the darkness. And the figure in the shadows followed.

In the world behind the fence the night seemed to have taken on another dimension. She was alone in that cold darkness. And all around her the wind soughed in lonely whispers as it crossed the waters of the estuary. Slowly, changes in the patterns of the shadows around her began to appear as her eyes became more accustomed to the night. And she became part of the darkness. Part of this place of evil.

What did she expect here? She looked around, as if in some way the answer lay in the fabric of the buildings. As indeed, it did.

She was crouching at the edge of an alley surrounded by rubble and broken glass. The alley ran between two tall buildings. One of them was built of Portland stone, with the steps leading up to a front portico supported by tall columns. Dimly, she could make out some of the letters set in the stone above the portico proclaiming the name of a long defunct city bank. The building on the other side of the alley was made of less ornate red brick, but it was still a substantial monument to what had been Garton's place in the world, and a brass plaque on the wall by the front door was engraved with the now barely discernible words -'*Garton Mission to Seamen*'.

For a moment she hesitated, afraid to leave the relative safety of the alley. Then the moon came from behind a bank of cloud, touching the scene with a silver sheen. In the light she could see a row of shops on the other side of the street. Some of them still had goods displayed in the windows, as if their owners had abandoned them in a hurry.

Suddenly something caught her eye. A movement somewhere in the row of shops. She froze, fighting the desire to scream.

There it was again. And this time she saw it. A bulky figure with a raised hand that stood in a shop doorway. She sensed danger and ran back into the alley, her breath coming in short sharp gasps as she focussed on the fact that someone was there in the night. For several minutes she forced herself to stand there and watch who, or whatever, it was. Until she realized the shop was an old fashioned tobacconist's emporium and the creature was standing in the doorway – a tall stuffed bear holding a large Meerschaum pipe in one of its paws.

Fiona moved out of the alley and crossed the street to the shops. She hurried past a greengrocers, an off-licence and a newsagents. The last shop in the row was a pharmacist. The window was broken, and a large glass bottle had crashed through onto the pavement where it lay surrounded by a coagulated yellow substance.

Round a corner a wall rose from the edge of the pavement and stretched backward to surround one of the houses. It was constructed of raw breeze block, topped by a concrete bulge embedded with reams of razor wire. The wall was an iconic image that had been carried by all the media. The '*Wall of Shame*' they'd named it, because of the unholy acts that had occurred within the house it isolated from the rest of the Waste Land. As if somehow the wall imprisoned the evil and kept it from the world outside.

Ahead of her, the mist rolled along the street, swirling in clouds trapped by the wall on one side and a terrace of tall Victorian houses on the other. As the mist came closer, Fiona felt herself being drawn to the house with the wall around it. It was a place that should have been destroyed, should have been ground into dust by the demolition men – consigning the memories to oblivion, and carrying with them the evil that had tainted the city.

She remembered the last time she'd been there. And she shivered – partly because of the mist coming in off the river, tinged with the thick smell of the black oily mud exposed by the retreating tide. Mainly, though, it was because of the fear eating away at her. She was linked to that evil, part of the story that had centred on that house. The house of the 'Toy Breaker'. Was that what the woman on the mobile had meant about Fiona 'being among friends', she wondered?

Suddenly, a soft wind came up the estuary and pushed the mist away as it disturbed the air. She heard the noise then. An insistent tap, tap, taping sound.

And it was coming from somewhere ahead where the row of shops ended. Next to them was a church, set behind bushes that fringed a low brick wall. An archway with a rotted wooden gate lead into the grounds of the church, and the tapping seemed to be coming from there. Steeling herself, Fiona moved towards the archway. She didn't feel brave. Far from it. And the only thing that stopped her fleeing was the knowledge that if she went back into the real world she'd be charged with murder.

The first thing she saw as she approached the gate was a wooden arch. A notice board was suspended from it, swinging from side to side in the wind. Tap, tap, tapping against the door frame. Which accounted for the noise she'd heard. She opened the gate and had starting to walk along a paved path to a side door when she saw the figure loom out of the murk.

It stood there, draped in a long hooded coat. Then it beckoned and went into the church.

'Wait,' Fiona called out. But nothing broke the silence of the darkness.

Torn between the possibility of losing the one person who might know what was going on, and the fear of entering the building, Fiona opted to follow the figure in the coat. Before she could change her mind, she moved along the path to the side door of the church. When she reached it she thought she saw a chink of light on the other side – a light that flickered in the darkness. The door opened easily enough as she pushed it, and she entered the church. Then she stood quite still, rooted to the spot.

There was no trace of the figure in the coat, but the area around the altar was lit by candles. Placed in a semi-circle, the flames were shivering now in the draught from the open door. In front of the candles, two glass-fronted picture frames were propped up against the step leading to the alter.

Each frame had a photograph inside it, and in the candle light Fiona recognized the people displayed in front of the alter. One was Adam Levine and the other was Debbie Connelly. Two patients who believed that Fiona had destroyed their lives.

Between the photographs someone had placed a piece of puppet theatre – a doll, wearing a strait-jacket and looking through the bars of a cage. When she looked closer Fiona saw there was a label tied around the doll's neck. When she bent forward to read the words on the label, Fiona felt a chill run through her.

Your turn now. And forever.

There it was. The final answer that the voice on the mobile had promised Fiona would find in the Waste Land. Everything had been set-up by Debbie Connelly and Adam Levine. And it was apparent now that they intended to make Fiona suffer as they'd suffered. And the message from the doll in the strait-jacket was clear. She would be locked away behind bars in a state-of-madness.

And the figure in the coat was lurking in the church right now.

Fiona turned and ran outside. She was bewildered by what she'd just witnessed, and wanted to get away and think. But time to think was a luxury that was denied her now because as she stumbled through the church gate there was a sudden flash of light, and someone called out. Then she saw a group of men running down the street towards her.

And the figure in the shadows cursed.

21

She looked around, desperate now. On the other side of the church two sheets of corrugated iron were nailed across the entrance to a narrow passage. Fiona ripped one of the sheets off and stepped into the alley. But she was surprised to be confronted by a modern looking green metal door secured by a heavy pad lock on a chain.

She'd walked into a trap.

For a moment panic grabbed her, freezing her to the spot. Then she saw there was a second passage to the side of the wall with the green door. It was a dank smelling narrow canyon that disappeared into the darkness, but Fiona was past caring now and she started to move down it. She almost tripped over as her foot caught against a pile of bricks lying on the ground. Then after a few yards the passage turned to the left and she was out into the moonlight as she entered a small yard. But any hope she had of taking refuge was dashed when she saw that the back door and the windows of the house in front of her were shuttered off with thick metal sheets. And the tops of the walls were protected with rolls of razor wire.

She cursed under her breath. The place was a fortress, and she realized there was only one reason why someone had gone to all the trouble of making an abandoned building so secure. It was a drug house, one of the places where the dealers played their trade.

As she stood there she remembered a seminar on drug dealers that she'd attended once. A police officer from Drug Squad had described several drug raids he'd been on, and one feature all the drug houses shared was that the dealers left themselves an escape route for emergencies. In derelict areas, where the dealers used old properties, a favourite route out was from house to house via the loft system. The police knew this, of course, but the dealers would set-up a series of hiding places along the routes they used. As the officer explained, it was an endless game in which sometimes the dealers got away with it and sometimes the law caught up with them. But the rewards were high enough to compensate for the risks.

Fiona decided that the people after her were probably drug dealers wondering who was invading their territory. Which meant they knew the area, and she didn't. For a moment she considered staying in the shadows and taking the chance that the people following her wouldn't know where she'd gone. But she realized it was a forlorn hope as she heard the sound of the corrugated iron sheets being pulled apart.

'Here.' The voice came out of the darkness and made Fiona's heart pound in shock. 'Follow me.'

It was a girl's voice and out of the corner of her eye Fiona saw a shadow come into view. For a moment she thought it was the figure in the coat, but then she saw it was a young woman who was dressed in an anorak and ski pants.

There was an old metal cooker against one wall of the yard and the girl climbed onto it. She balanced there for a moment, before pulling off her anorak and laying it down across the razor wire on top of the wall. Then she beckoned to Fiona and helped her onto the cooker, before levering herself over the top of the wall and jumping down. Fiona followed her, yanking the anorak free as she did so. She landed on the paving stones of the yard next door and gave the girl her jacket back

The figure in the coat waited, then followed at a discreet distance.

The girl took Fiona's hand and pulled her across the yard to the back door of the house. There were no fortifications here and the door opened with a soft creaking sound when the girl pushed it. Then she drew Fiona inside. They were in the remains of a kitchen with a cracked ceramic sink in one corner. A grey light came in through a broken window, and the girl crossed the kitchen to a lobby on the far side of the room. The passage led to a flight of stairs at the far end. The girl climbed the stairs and came out on a small landing. It was dark up there but Fiona could dimly see the outline of a square trapdoor in the ceiling.

On the landing a small chest of drawers was against one of the walls, and the girl positioned it under the trapdoor. Then she climbed on top and pushed the trapdoor to one side. By levering her hands on the edge of the gap she was able to swing herself into the roof space. She leaned forward and helped Fiona to join her.

They were in a loft and by the dim light that filtered through a dirty skylight Fiona saw that holes had been knocked into both end walls. The girl led the way to the hole on the right, careful to keep her feet on the cross beams, and ducked through the opening. The loft space beyond had a clean skylight and a plywood floor. An electric cable ran along the roof joists and there was a stack of metal shelves along the back wall, with a long bench in front of them. The shelves contained plastic bags full of white power, and there was a balance and a tray of instruments on the bench.

On the far side of the loft another hole had been knocked into the wall, and in the pale light Fiona could see a rolled up ladder on the floor next to it. The girl secured one end of the ladder to hooks driven into the floor boards, tossed the other end out of the hole and disappeared after it. Then she threw the ladder back up and Fiona followed her. When she reached the ground the girl was already standing by an archway and she waited until Fiona joined her. Then she took Fiona's hand and guided her through a bewildering maze of dark alleys and open spaces until she came to a small square with a park in the centre. She crossed the grass and led Fiona round to the back of one of the houses and down a flight of steps to a heavy wooden door.

She unlocked it, pushed it open and led Fiona inside. There was a table against one wall with a torch on it. The girl switched on the torch, shut the door and led Fiona along a passage which opened up into a large room.

'Hold that, please.' She passed the torch to Fiona and lit an oil lamp on a table in the centre of the room.

'There. That's better. Now tell me what you were doing in the Waste Land at this time of night?'

Outside, the figure in the coat stayed in the shadows. Watching the house.

22

'What the hell's going on?' For a moment Falcon felt he was being squeezed in a vice. 'Are we saying Fiona committed the murder of a young woman down at the docks? A murder caught on CCTV?'

Loxley had called an emergency briefing and Falcon, Goldilocks and Carl Lucas were with him in the operation room.

'It looks that way, sir.' Goldilocks said, sounding distraught.

'Is the dock sealed off?' Loxley asked, trying to force some kind of practicality into the proceedings.

'Yes, the whole area's a crime scene while we try to establish if that woman on the CCTV footage was actually killed and dumped in the dock.'

'And Fiona?'

'She's disappeared. Her car's still in her garage at the apartment block, but there's no sign of Fiona herself.'

'OK. Fiona's out there on the run.' Loxley turned to Lucas. 'So what's your take on recent developments?'

Lucas nodded, acknowledging that in Fiona's absence he would be answering questions she would have been expected to field. And the irony wasn't lost on him that most of the questions coming in would be about Fiona herself.

'It seems to me that the CCTV murder was staged with one aim in mind and one only – to ratchet up the pressure on Fiona. That's why it was plastered all over the media, so Fiona would feel she was being trapped in a corner.'

'You make it sound like a game,' Goldilocks snapped.

'Oh, it's game all right. A very serious game. We can be certain of that.' Lucas replied, in no way fazed by the sergeant's manner.

'Sorry, I'm a bit on edge,' Goldilocks apologized. 'Don't forget, Fiona was in my charge. But I don't understand what's happening here. The CCTV showed her pounding that girl's head with a rock. But what could turn Fiona into a killer like that? I've known her for years, and she's such a warm, gentle person.'

'That is a puzzle, I agree.' Lucas nodded. 'It's almost as if....'

'As if what?' Falcon prompted him.

'As if someone is trying to change that gentle personality. To make Fiona into something she isn't. Or at least into something she shouldn't be.'

'Is that possible?' Loxley sounded unconvinced.

'Put enough stress on someone and yes, it could affect their personality traits. And, as I said just now, the whole point of the CCTV murder was to increase the pressure on Fiona, by turning her into a murderer. Think about it. Somehow Fiona was made to kill that girl. Then the murder was shown on terrestrial TV, and Fiona was left with only two options. Either turn herself in to the police, or become an outcast on the run. Can you imagine what that must have done to her mental state?'

'It must have torn her apart?' It was Goldilocks who answered him.

'Right. Just as planned. But at least we don't have to try to predict what she will do next,' Lucas said, 'because it looks very much as if she's already made her choice. She's gone on the run. We know that because she clobbered the officer who was protecting her. But her car's still in her garage, so she's probably stayed local among the places she knows.'

'So what will she do now?' Falcon asked. 'For the moment she's got away. But it's very lonely out there. How will she cope with that?'

Lucas turned to him. 'You know her better than I do. How strong is she mentally?'

'That's the problem.' Falcon sighed. 'Up to a year or so ago, I would have said she was solid as a rock. Now, after the affair with the glass lift, I'm not so sure. I don't think she's fully recovered from what happened yet.'

'So she's vulnerable.'

'I think she is, yes.' Falcon replied, 'which makes it important to second guess what she will do now she's on the run.'

'There's a problem there, I'm afraid,' Lucas said. 'Because I don't think she'll know herself what she intends to do. Going on the run was almost certainly an instinctive spur of the moment reaction. When she stops and thinks, she'll see that. And that's when the panic could really start to kick in.'

'And she's out there on the run,' Goldilocks added, 'believing everyone's against her.'

'Oh my God.' Carl Lucas suddenly snapped his fingers.

'What is it?' Goldilocks asked, anxiety evident in her voice.

'I think I've just realized what this is all about. I missed it earlier, when I said it was almost as if someone was trying to change Fiona's gentle personality into something else.'

'So?' Loxley tried not to sound impatient.

'So someone, we think it's Debbie Connelly, *is* trying to do just that. And everything makes sense now. A sequence of events was initiated with the intention of eating away at Fiona's mind which, don't forget, was already vulnerable. First, there was the incident at the fountain, and then she was snatched from her apartment and taken to the vagrant camp, where she *lost* two hours. And finally, and we don't know how yet, she was coerced in to committing the CCTV murder. After that, everything moves up a gear. And what started as an investigation to protect Fiona now becomes a murder inquiry – with her as the prime suspect. And however clever she is at evading capture, she will be caught in the end. True?'

'True,' Loxley agreed.

'But it's the motive we missed out on. I believe that whoever is running this, wants to exact the ultimate vengeance.'

'The ultimate vengeance?' Goldilocks breathed the words. 'What's that?'

'I think I know now. Whoever's responsible for this wants Fiona to suffer the full extent of what they themselves suffered. And there's only one way to make that happen.'

'And what's that?' Falcon asked.

'To have Fiona charged with the murder on the basis of the CCTV footage, but found unfit to plead on the basis of her mental state.'

'Then she'll be locked away in a secure psychiatric clinic.' Goldilocks could hardly say the words.

'I believe that's what their twisted minds want. And to achieve it, they need to finally drive Fiona mad.' Lucas sounded bleak.

'By increasing the pressure on her to an even higher level?' Loxley asked.

'I fear so. I said just now that a sequence of events had been initiated. Well, I believe there's one final incident in that sequence still to be staged. Something waiting out there that's terrifying enough to tip Fiona over the edge.'

23

There was a long silence as they tried to come to terms with what Lucas had told them.

In the end, Goldilocks shook her head. 'It's evil. Pure evil. Shutting someone away like that in a mental home. It just doesn't bear thinking about.'

'But at least we've identified what we believe to be the motive behind all this,' Loxley said. 'Debbie Connelly wants Fiona committed to a mental institution to suffer as she herself suffered at the hands of the psychiatrists.'

'I agree with that.' Falcon dragged his thoughts back from the dark place where they'd strayed. 'The preferred option is to reduce Fiona to such a state that she *will* be committed to an institution. But if that fails, Debbie Connelly will have the perfect fall-back position. If Fiona stays sane, she'll be charged and almost certainly found guilty of murder – which means a long time behind bars.'

Loxley turned to Falcon. 'Time to step back and take stock before we work out our next move. How did everything kick off today?'

'We have two main witnesses,' Falcon replied. 'The reporter at Vista TV, John Harris, who was approached with the offer of the CCTV footage, and the manager of the unit that monitors the CCTV for the ferry terminal. We can sketch in the details from what they've told us, but everything we've got at the moment is preliminary and is being constantly updated.'

Falcon paused, gathering his thoughts. 'Apparently, there was a phone call made by a woman to the main desk at the Vista TV studios at around 4.30 p.m. this afternoon. The caller told the desk that she had information on a murder that had taken place the night before. At that stage, she was referred to John Harris and she told him the murder had been recorded on CCTV footage taken at the entrance to the ferry terminal buildings by the docks. Then she dropped the bombshell and told Harris that the killer was Fiona Nightingale – an offender profiler used by the Garton police. And of course, as far as Harris was concerned, that moved the incident into the big league.'

'I bet it did,' Goldilocks said. 'So the reporter took the caller seriously after that?'

'Seriously enough to look into what she'd told him. And the first thing he wanted to know was how she'd got hold of the CCTV material? At first, the caller seemed reluctant to reveal any details about that. But then Harris explained that without convincing verification he couldn't proceed with the story since she might just be wasting his time. So she explained how she got hold of the CCTV footage. She paid for it.'

'You mean it was released to her for cash, just like that?' Goldilocks asked.

'Well,' Falcon shrugged, 'it's not quite as bad as it sounds. According to Harris, the security they employ at the ferry terminal is an unmonitored incidence-response system that changes during the hours of darkness. Most of the time it's in passive mode. But it activates if the alarms at the entrance to the ferry building are triggered by an incident. At that stage, the scanning control of the CCTV camera passes to the monitoring centre and if needed an operator can send out a response unit – either one of their own, or one from the police. The rest of the time, the CCTV footage is unmonitored and simply repeats itself on an "hours of darkness" cycle.'

'But what if the images from the camera are needed?' Loxley asked.

'They have a system that can transfer the data from the disc in the camera to a disc in the monitoring centre. The data can then be retrieved if there's a requirement for it. And according to the manager of the centre that's what happened when the woman went to see him. Her boyfriend was with her, and she explained that it had been his stag party in a dockland club. The girl had come to drive him home later that night, but when they got to the ferry terminal her boyfriend's mates played a final joke on him. Apparently, they stripped him, poured oil over his body and covered him with feathers. But they'd left him his clothes, and after he'd cleaned up he and his girlfriend went to the monitoring booth. They told the night manager that they both thought it was very funny and wanted a copy of the CCTV footage as a wedding souvenir. They offered the manager a hundred pounds for a copy. The manager told them he wanted to look at the footage before he was prepared to release it, but the boyfriend said he was too embarrassed and since he wanted the money the manager didn't push it.'

'So he had no real idea what was on the disc he sold to the couple?' Loxley said.

'No, but the security alarms are only triggered if the doors to the ferry terminal are directly threatened, and since they weren't set off in this case, the manager didn't think it would matter what was on the disc because it would be wiped clear at the end of the night shift and reused without being looked at because there was no reason to check what was on it. No, as far as the manager was concerned, it was a chance to make a few bob.'

'And the original disc would have been wiped clean at the end of the night shift,' Loxley said. 'But there is something we can pick up here. Fiona had already told us that two people were involved when she was snatched from her apartment. Now two people were involved in buying the disc. More evidence that our prime suspect, Debbie Connelly, has an accomplice. And my guess is it was Adam Devine both times.'

'But why didn't Debbie Connelly just hand the CCTV disc to the police in the first place?' Goldilocks asked.

'Maximum exposure,' Lucas replied. 'According to Harris, the woman who held the disc wanted it shown on TV, but only at the time she stipulated.'

'Why the special time?' Falcon was thinking aloud, but no one answered him.

Instead, Loxley took up another point. 'According to Harris, he wanted a face-to-face meeting with the caller, but she refused. She said that she would send the disc to the Vista office by courier, in time to be shown on a specific local news slot that she would stipulate. And here the caller was very clever. She said she was offering the disc to Vista as an exclusive, but that she had a copy of it and if they didn't put the footage out on the particular slot, she would release the disc to the rest of the media.'

'So that's the way the caller got to control the time at which the disc was shown on air. But why bother with a particular time slot?' Goldilocks pushed Falcon's question.

'To build up the pressure on Fiona, I'm afraid,' Lucas answered. 'And with the information supplied by the officer outside Fiona's flat I think we can see the way it worked now. True, there was no way the suspects could control the time at which Fiona left the hospital. But all they had to do was wait until she arrived at the apartment block, and on that basis select the time slot they wanted and tell the TV company. Vista already had a copy of the disc, remember, but unless they put it out when they were told it would no longer be an exclusive.'

'Neat,' Falcon agreed.

'So, after Vista were told the slot, a copy of the disc was delivered to the security desk at Fiona's apartment block a few minutes before it was to be broadcast. The security officer phoned Fiona and told her a package was waiting for her, and the bobby outside her door went and collected it. And when he'd checked that it was no more than a DVD in a plastic cover, he passed it on to Fiona.'

'Sounds plausible.' Loxley nodded. 'So we can assume that Fiona saw a copy of the CCTV footage just before it went out on air.'

'Right,' Lucas agreed. 'Which is why she was panicked into going on the run. Or maybe, Debbie Connelly contacted Fiona at the apartment and told her the police would be coming after her. Anyway, for whatever reason she went on the run.'

'But that means she was free. Lost to both Debbie Connelly *and* the police,' Loxley said.

'Not necessarily.' Falcon snapped his fingers. 'Debbie Connelly could have been watching the apartment, and then followed Fiona when she left. That way she could keep tabs on her.'

'You mean they didn't mind that Fiona was on the run?' Goldilocks asked.

'Absolutely not,' Lucas said, shaking his head. 'If they were following her they could reel her in anytime. Meanwhile the pressure on her would be increasing all the time. And I think this strengthens the argument that Debbie Connelly has planned a final incident for Fiona. Otherwise, why not just turn her over to the police for the CCTV murder?'

At that moment a red light flashed on the console, and Goldilocks lifted the receiver. She listened for a moment, thanked the caller, and put the receiver down. Then she turned to Loxley. 'That was the officer sent round to the CCTV Monitoring Centre with photographs of our two suspects. The night manager who was on duty confirmed from the pictures that Debbie Connelly and Adam Devine were the two people he sold the disc to.'

'Got 'em.' Loxley expelled his breath. 'Now we can be certain who we're chasing.'

'True,' Falcon agreed. 'Problem is, now we're chasing Fiona as well. On a charge of murder.'

24

There was a long silence in the room that was finally broken by Loxley.

'And she *did* commit the murder. We watched her do it on the CCTV footage,' he said, pushing the point.

'Yes,' Falcon almost snapped back at his superior. Then he seemed to recover, but he sounded down. 'We've seen the murder being committed – along with millions of TV viewers.'

'What about the disc now. Where is it?' Loxley asked.

'The original? I don't know,' Goldilocks answered. 'But Harris supplied us with a copy; although he was careful to make sure it didn't arrive at police HQ before the news went out.'

'Where's the copy now?' Falcon asked.

'After we viewed it, I sent it to the techies,' Goldilocks said. 'Arthur Fielding's running checks on it and he'll be in touch as soon as he has anything.'

'So for the moment, we just wait around.' Falcon was obviously feeling frustrated.

'Look, Gary.' Loxley sounded impatient, although he was keeping a lid on it. 'I know Fiona's a friend of yours. But this is a murder inquiry now and we have to go by the book. And perhaps we also have to finally accept that Fiona's gone off the rails. God knows she's been under enough stress these last few days.'

Was he deliberately distancing himself from Fiona, Falcon wondered? Was it possible he was afraid of guilt by association? Worried that some of the dirt might rub off on him as senior investigating officer if Fiona was found guilty of murder? Falcon had seen that fear blight detectives' records in the past.

Or was it something else? Loxley had more or less been conciliatory when Falcon had pushed to keep Fiona's case up there with that of the supposed serial killer. But now the superintendent was coming down hard on Fiona, and in doing so he was subtly changing the dynamic of the investigation, making it quite clear that from now on they were dealing with Fiona the murderer – not with Fiona the friend.

But Falcon let none of his worries show. If he was going to lock horns with Loxley, this wasn't the ground to fight over. Not with Fiona looking as guilty as hell.

'Fiona's a friend of a lot of officers in CID. Not just me.' Falcon forced himself to stay calm. 'But that doesn't buy her any favours. It's just that I can't believe that she could have killed that woman.'

'You've seen the CCTV footage on the disc. It was Fiona who was caught on camera,' Loxley said, the words sounding harsh and with no trace of sympathy. 'And according to the time on the disc, the murder was carried out during the two hours Fiona went missing—' Loxley was interrupted as a female officer came up to him.

'Report just in from the ferry terminal, Sir. A body matching the description of the woman thrown into the water has been found trapped under the pier where the ferries dock. Apparently one of the officers there recognized her. She was a druggie who lived rough in the dock area.'

'So it's officially a murder inquiry now.'

To Falcon, Loxley's tone seemed even harsher.

25

The oil lamp threw shadows across the walls. The room was furnished in a curiously old-fashioned style, with heavy dark wood furniture and a chintz-covered three piece suite.

'OK, so why are you in the Waste Land on your own?' The girl repeated the question.

For a moment Fiona thought of telling her to mind her own business. But she realized that the woman sounded genuinely interested, not aggressive.

'I came here looking for answers.'

'Answers to what?'

When Fiona didn't reply the woman asked if she'd like some tea.

'Actually, I wouldn't mind something a bit stronger.'

The woman grinned. 'G and T all right?'

'Perfect.'

'Then I'll join you. And my name's Petra, by the way.' She was dressed like a hippy, with her blonde hair in a pigtail.

'Fiona.'

'OK, Fiona, I'll get us those drinks.'

Petra went into another room and when she came back she was carrying a tray with glasses and two bottles on it. She twisted the screw-top off the green bottle and poured two generous measures of gin into the glasses. Then she topped them up with tonic from the other bottle that had ice cold condensation running down the sides.

'Oh, yes.' Petra smiled as she noticed Fiona's apparent surprise. 'All mod cons here. Including a battery-driven fridge. So what shall we drink to?'

'How about you rescuing me from those men?'

'Right. Cheers.' Petra lifted her glass in a mock salute. 'Although to be perfectly honest, I don't think they meant you any real harm once they realized you were with me.'

'They're friends of yours?'

'No.' The word was almost spat out. 'They're drug dealers. But they tolerate us being here.'

'Us?'

'My partner and I.'

'Why do they tolerate you?'

'We frighten people away,' she said enigmatically. 'Anyone foolish enough to come to the Waste Land, that is.'

'What do you mean, you "frighten people away"?' Fiona asked.

But instead of replying, Petra rephrased her earlier question.

'What kind of answers were you looking for at the drug house? You obviously weren't there to do business with the dealers because they were after you. So?'

It was a stand-off. But for some reason she didn't altogether understand, Fiona trusted this woman. And, in any case, she thought, where else could she go?

'Where to start?'

'Try the old cliché. At the beginning.'

Fiona sipped her drink, then put the glass down and told Petra everything that had happened over the past few days, and how it related to the past.

'So that's it. Warts and all.' She sat back, waiting for a reaction.

For a long moment, there was silence. Then Petra smiled. 'Too far-fetched to be a lie. So, bottom line. Did you commit that murder?'

Fiona felt the despair again. 'That's the whole point, Petra. I don't know. I can't remember doing it, and I don't think I'm the kind of person to commit murder either. But I was drugged and open to suggestion, and there's a missing window of two hours on the night that girl was killed at the ferry terminal. And worst of all, I was captured carrying out the murder on CCTV. So I don't know what to believe any more.'

'The murder was caught on CCTV and then shown on the telly. God, whoever's behind this has really got in for you, haven't they?'

'Looks that way.'

'And you're not prepared to go to the police?'

'Not at this stage, no. I still can't believe I would have committed murder, but until I can fill in those missing two hours my hands are tied. And that's why I came to the Waste Land. Because one of the vagrants round the oil drum told me I'd been brought here by a woman on the night of the murder.'

'But I don't understand. What did you hope to find here in this derelict place?'

'I don't know. But originally I must have been brought here for a reason. So I thought that maybe I would remember something.'

'And did you?'

'No.' Fiona felt the panic rising again. 'But I was being led on.'

'What do you mean, led on?'

'There was a figure in a long coat and hood, and it beckoned me into a derelict church to see a display in front of the alter.'

'What kind of display?'

Fiona told her about the photographs and the doll in a strait-jacket.

'Weird.'

'You mean, you don't believe me?'

'Like I said before, this is too fantastic not to be true. But right now you're no closer to finding the killer, are you?'

'No. The only positive information I obtained was that on the night of the murder, a woman brought me to the vagrant's pitch by the river, and from there took me into the Waste Land. And it looks as if the same woman was inside the Waste Land tonight.'

'OK, not a lot. But I might just be able to help you.'

'But why should you help someone on the run from the police?'

Petra smiled. 'Well, for one thing, you don't strike me as a murderer.'

'So how do you think you can help?'

'Let me explain. I'm part of a team that runs a drop-in centre for the homeless. It's located in what used to be an old seaman's shelter at the south end of the docks. We also have a caravan that moves from site to site. Over the years the drifters, as I like to call them, have come to trust the members of the team. So maybe they'll talk to me.'

'It's worth a try, I suppose.'

'But?' Petra looked at her closely.

'You have to admit that it's a bit strange. You living like this in a condemned section of the town.'

'Yes.' Petra sighed. For a moment Fiona thought she wasn't going to say anymore. Then she smiled. 'I do have a place on the outside. But this is my home now.'

'You choose to live here? Why?'

'Because the stupid girl thinks she wants to spend her life with me.'

Fiona gasped as a figure appeared out of the darkness.

Outside in the shadows, the figure in the long coat watched the man enter the house.

And the tears came then. Long wracking sobs.

26

He was tall and slim, with a mass of dark curly hair. And his face was covered in a skin-coloured resin mask.

Petra ran across to him and buried her face in his shoulder. He stroked her hair then gently pulled her away. 'Aren't you going to introduce us, Petra?'

'Fiona this is my partner, Greg Harker. He's been away for a couple of days. Greg, this is Fiona.'

'Fiona. I have to say I was lurking in the passage listening to the two of you. So I got most of what you said.'

'Including the bit about me being on the run for murder.'

'All that, yes.'

'You know about the murder?'

'The girl who was dumped in the dock? Yes. It's been the talk of the vagrant community. As much as they talk about anything, that is. And now you're saying the police believe you are the murderer?'

'Yes. I was even caught on CCTV doing it.'

'Excuse me.' He left the room and when he returned he was holding an opened can of beer. 'You know, somehow the murder of a vagrant makes a kind of sense.'

'How do you mean?' Fiona asked him.

'The situation among the vagrants has been odd for the past few months or so. I've never known them to be so nervy. So on edge.'

'Perhaps I should explain Greg's position in all this.' Petra looked across at Greg who nodded.

'I first met Greg over a year ago when he came to the drop-in centre which is run by the charity I work for. He was wearing the mask, and it was soon obvious that he was a very disturbed person. For the first few weeks he kept himself very much to himself, but eventually he started to talk to me, and bit by bit it all came out. Greg had been in a motorcycle crash and suffered extensive burns to his face. Hence the mask.'

'I was in a bad way,' Greg interrupted. 'I'd had therapy, but it really didn't do any good. I still felt abandoned. And I made it worse by isolating myself from society, and moving from place to place through the vagrant communities in the big cities. But then I met Petra and she gave me hope. At first, I thought what she felt was pity. But I was wrong. For some reason I don't understand she accepted me for what I was.'

Petra took his hand and held it. 'Greg's learning to come to terms with the past. For the moment, he helps me in the caravan the charity runs for vagrants. And he does a useful job, because they've learned to trust him. Some of them even turn to him for help. We just have the one ground rule in our relationship. I'm not allowed to see his face. Not yet anyway.'

'It had to be that way,' Greg said. 'If Petra actually saw my face then there would be no room for pretending any more. I could fool myself that Petra could love me, yes. But only if she never saw what was left of my face. Does that make sense?'

'Oddly enough, it does,' Fiona replied. 'I'm a psychiatrist and I've treated patients who've felt the same way towards burns they'd suffered. Keep the effects hidden, and they could be accepted. Reveal the extent of the injuries, and the game's up. The fragile screen they'd built around themselves has collapsed.'

'That was just how I felt. Which is why we put down the ground rule. For now, my face stays hidden.' Greg finished off the can of beer.

'So you came to the Waste Land to set-up house together.'

'Temporarily, yes,' Greg replied. 'I still couldn't face living in society, and in that sense, the Waste Land was ideal for me. No one except the drug dealers come here, and even they restrict themselves to one corner of the place. At first, I lived on an old tugboat tied up at an abandoned landing stage. But after I got to know Petra we moved in here.'

'OK, but why do the dealers restrict themselves to just one part of the Waste Land? I should have thought it was an ideal place for them to set up a base using more of the derelict buildings. So why pass up the chance?'

'It's quite simple, really,' Petra answered. 'The Toy Breaker connection.'

'The Toy Breaker.' Fiona repeated the words softly, so low the words were hardly audible. 'Of course.'

'You know about The Toy Breaker?' Petra asked.

'Oh, yes, I know about The Toy Breaker. Carol Devril. The nurse who killed all those babies. In fact, I worked the case with the Garton police. When it was all over the house where The Toy Breaker lived was to be raised to the ground. Not unusual in these circumstances. For one thing, it keeps the tourists away. The house was to go as part of a docks clearance scheme. But it was a private development and the parent company ran out of money before they could even start on the demolition stage. And the house is still there.'

'That's right, it is,' Petra said. 'But it's become a symbol of evil. There's even suggestions that ghosts have been seen there. So now even the drug dealers give it a wide birth,' Petra said.

'You worked the case,' Greg said. 'And now you've been drawn back onto the Waste Land. The place where the Toy Breaker lived. Quite a coincidence, don't you think?'

'You mean you don't believe it is a coincidence?' Fiona asked.

He shrugged. 'Someone wanted to finger you for the CCTV murder, and it seems to me that whoever it is has drawn you here. First to the vagrants, then inside the Waste Land itself. Why?'

Fiona shrugged listlessly. 'I don't know.'

'What made you want to come into the Waste Land in the first place?'

Fiona thought for a moment, trying to clear her mind of the drug residues.

'It was a suggestion made in a letter written by Debbie Connelly, the woman running the campaign against me.'

'And how did you know how to get here?'

'One of the vagrants led me into the Waste Land in exchange for a twenty pound note.'

'And then what? You just wandered around until Petra found you?'

'Yes.'

'So you saw nothing in the Waste Land to indicate why you'd been drawn here?'

'Yes, I did. The church: candles were lit inside, and there were two photographs by the altar.'

'Photographs of who?' Greg asked, suddenly alert.

'Of the two people who have been tormenting me – Debbie Connelly and Adam Devine.'

'Anything else?' Petra asked.

'Yes, I remember now. There was a scene from a puppet show. A girl wearing a strait-jacket looking out through the bars of a prison.'

'What a strange thing,' Petra said.

'Not really,' Fiona replied. 'I imagine it was there to represent my future as a murderer.'

'Prison behind bars, yes,' Petra persisted. 'But why the strait-jacket?'

Fiona shrugged. 'Who knows the way Debbie Connelly's mind works.'

'You were deliberately drawn to the Waste Land,' Greg said. 'And when you get here you find the display in the church – obviously put on for your benefit. So what else is in store?'

'I've no idea,' Fiona said, sounding listless.

'Leave it with me. I'll talk to the vagrants and find out if they've seen any extra activity around the area. They more or less trust me, and they might just talk. Meanwhile, I suggest you stay here with Petra until it's safe to go back to the outside and face the music.'

Fiona agreed, but she couldn't help wondering if it would ever be safe to go back.

27

The team met again in the operations room at noon the next day to report progress on the hunt for Fiona. Loxley, Falcon, and Goldilocks were present, but Carl Lucas was late, and when he joined the others a few minutes later he apologized.

'I've had another contact,' he said.

'How did they reach you this time?' Loxley asked.

'A message was left with *Vista TV* in an envelope addressed to me. *Vista* called me and that's where I've been. Picking up the letter.'

'Who delivered it to *Vista TV*?'

'Don't know. Apparently, the girl on reception was busy with an incoming phone call, and the visitor just dumped the letter on the desk and left. But the girl thinks the visitor was wearing a long coat.'

'Have you read the letter?' Falcon asked.

'No. I thought it best to bring it here before opening it. '

'I don't suppose the envelope's sterile?' Falcon asked.

'No,' Loxley replied. 'Too many people have already handled it. But unlike the first letter, this one's not been opened. So maybe we can get a decent DNA profile from it.'

'I'll see to it.' Goldilocks walked across the room and came back carrying a tray with an assortment of plastic instruments, latex gloves and evidence bags on it. She put the tray down on the work surface, pulled on a pair of Latex gloves and opened two evidence bags. Then she slit the envelope with a paper knife from the tray and used a pair of tweezers to lift out the single sheet of paper inside. She placed the envelope and the paper into separate evidence bags then sealed and labelled them.

'OK.' Loxley turned to Lucas. 'Can you read out the letter to us, please?'

Lucas put on a pair of gloves, and Goldilocks took the letter from its evidence bag and passed it to him. Lucas scanned the text for a moment then began to read it out loud.

Janus Man

Another letter for your collection. Our friend Fiona is completely in my power now. I can make her do anything I want to. Even to committing murder.

I control her. You know that.

But now I'm not the only one after her, am I? The police have joined the chase for the murderer. Sorry, I mean for their 'little princess'. And I do like to see the plod running round like headless chickens.

But enough is enough, isn't it? Dear little Fiona's time on the run will soon be up. So do I know what she will do next? Oh, yes, I know. We're ready to move forward, and you will see it unfold, Janus Man. So I'll give you another teeny weenie clue.

To start off, you should tell the plod to look more closely at the less fortunate in our caring society.

'There are at least two important pieces of information in this letter,' Falcon said, when Carl Lucas had finished reading it out. 'First off, we know now that Debbie Connelly, who we'll assume wrote the letter, isn't holding Fiona. So it appears she's still on the run from both sides.

'Next,' Falcon went on. 'The letter seems to be directing us to the "less fortunate" in society. Which probably means the vagrants, because don't forget the murdered girl was part of the Garton vagrant community. So Fiona must have had some connection with them.'

'But why push us towards them?' Goldilocks asked. 'It doesn't make sense.'

'It does if Debbie wants us to see how everything develops,' Carl Lucas said. 'She'll feed us just enough to keep us involved—'

He was interrupted as Arthur Fielding, head of Scene of Crimes came into the room.

'So what have you got for us, Arthur?' Falcon asked.

Arthur Fielding cleared his throat, relishing his small moment of drama.

'We carried out a series of tests on the material displayed on the CCTV disc. It will be several hours before the tests are complete, but I thought you'd like a progress report.'

He held up the disc he'd brought with him. 'The item of interest to us only runs for around three minutes, so we isolated the relevant footage and made a few adjustments to the original.'

He put the disc he was carrying into the tray of one of the DVD players in the room and pressed the play button.

'This first sequence is a straight copy of the original footage, and you can see the entrance to the ferry terminal in the background, and the figures in front of it.'

As they watched, the images shown on TV earlier that evening came up on the screen.

'OK,' Arthur Fielding said. 'That was the sequence that allowed us to make a visual identification of Fiona as the CCTV killer. Then we brought in the standard facial recognition programme we use. We had on record photos of Fiona taken after her accident, showing her facial scars – the photos were taken in case they might be needed if Fiona went after compensation – and we compared these photos with images taken from the CCTV footage.'

'And?' Loxley fought to curb his impatience.

'The main feature on both sets of photos is the scarring that's found on the left side of Fiona's face.'

'So the face caught on CCTV is Fiona's ?' Falcon asked.

'It was a match, yes. But we ran more tests. Look.' He ran another sequence on the screen. 'Here we cleaned up the background and sharpened the images. And this time we enlarged the face of the woman in the long coat. We did our best, but I'm afraid it's not wedding photo class. Still, see what you make of it.'

He fast forwarded the disc then stopped it at the point where an image of the woman in the long coat came into view. For a moment it almost looked as if she was deliberately posing for the camera as Arthur Fielding froze the image on the screen.

The silence was drawn out this time as they gazed at the image of the face.

Then Goldilocks let out her breath, 'It is Fiona? No doubt about it. Look at the scars on her cheeks. They've not healed completely yet.'

'It looks like Fiona, I agree,' Fielding said. 'But at this point in time, we're testing an advanced facial recognition system with state of the art software. It lets us alter a variety of parameters on images, with quite remarkable results. For instance, look at this.'

He brought another image onto the screen. 'This is the face without the scars.'

The image had changed completely now.

'And this is the same face with the shape of the nose modified.'

Again, the difference was amazing.

'So what are you saying, Arthur?' Falcon asked.

'We ran the CCTV footage through the new facial recognition programme and checked it against Fiona's image.'

'And?' Loxley was watching him carefully now.

'And the woman on the CCTV sequence is *not* Fiona Nightingale.'

'Phew,' Goldilocks let her breath out. 'Thank God for that. But I still don't understand. Surely whoever set this up would realize that we would find out the CCTV footage had been faked?'

'No,' Arthur Fielding replied. 'Remember, the original facial recognition programme found a match. It was only when we used the programme we were testing that we found it wasn't Fiona's face. Nonetheless, who ever put this in place was a make-up expert. The best.'

'Makes sense,' Goldilocks said. 'Our prime suspect was an actress. Changing character with cosmetics would have been second nature to her.'

'So, let's say she applied the make up to her own face, and took the place of Fiona, in the murder sequence. But the make-up wasn't good enough to fool the computer programme you were testing?' Falcon said.

'No, it wasn't good enough,' Arthur Fielding replied. 'The programme rejected Fiona's face as a match to that of the killer. And when we looked closely we could see why. The make-up artist had used very modern cosmetics, including artificial skin and flesh, to replicate the scars and the shapes of Fiona's nose and cheeks. You might even say it was a work of art. Even so, it didn't fool the new programme. But it was pure luck that we were testing it at the time.'

'Otherwise we'd have accepted it was Fiona's face,' Goldilocks said.

'Yes,' Arthur Fielding nodded. 'And I'd guess your prime suspect thought that because the face looked like Fiona's, it would be accepted as being Fiona's.'

'So, bottom line, the new programme can tell it's not Fiona's face? Even with images as poor as this?' Loxley asked.

'It can do better than that. It can tell you whose face it really is. Someone else who was already on our database.'

'And who's that?' Falcon asked.

'Debbie Connelly. The woman who tried to kill Fiona in the glass lift.'

28

Debbie Connelly.

Loxley began to pace the floor. 'So, together with the identification the CCTV manager made from the photographs, we have irrefutable proof that Debbie Connelly is driving the attacks on Fiona, proving we were right to flag her as the prime suspect.'

'Right,' Falcon agreed. 'But we know now that Fiona wasn't the CCTV killer. So why did she run?' He looked at Carl Lucas.

'Because she'd seen the CCTV recording and believed that she *was* the killer because of the evidence against her on the disc. And she knew the police would see it that way. So put yourself in her place. She was frightened and alone, and in her state of mind I think she must have come to the conclusion that the only way left to her was to go on the run and try to find out what really happened the night of the murder.'

'You think she's gone looking for answers, rather than just hiding away?' Falcon asked.

Lucas shrugged. 'It depends entirely on her state of mind. What would the old Fiona have done?'

'No question,' Falcon answered. 'She'd have fought back. But surely she must have known she didn't kill that woman.' Falcon persisted with the question.

'Not necessarily,' Carl Lucas replied. 'We could be dealing with very special conditions here. Remember, Fiona had been drugged and that could have left her in a confused state that could easily have impaired her judgement and maybe made her believe anything. Like I said, everything depends on her state of mind.'

'But there's something else here, isn't there?' Falcon said.

'And what's that?' Lucas asked.

'A girl was killed in the incident at the ferry terminal, so if it was designed to finger Fiona for murder then it was a very elaborate set-up. Would Debbie Connelly really go to the lengths of actually killing that girl, just to get at Fiona?'

'Yes,' Lucas came in again. 'If she hated Fiona enough, and wanted her to suffer. And don't forget, the CCTV incident was meant to prove that Fiona was the killer. And to do that, a body was needed. So, yes, I'd say Debbie Connelly would sacrifice the vagrant girl to provide a murder victim. Particularly if everybody, including the police, believed Fiona had committed the murder. It was just Debbie Connelly's misfortune that SOCO were testing this state-of-the-art facial recognition programme.'

'So how do we move forward?' Loxley asked Falcon.

'Debbie Connelly doesn't know Fiona's in the clear for the CCTV murder, so for her nothing's changed. As far as she is concerned, Fiona is still on the run. So we keep shtum about the CCTV murder. And then we sharpen up the hunt for Fiona. We have to find her before Debbie Connelly does, because God knows what she'll do to Fiona if she finds out that her plans for vengeance are in tatters.'

'And right now, we have no idea where Fiona is,' Falcon cut in. 'We know she left her apartment because she knocked the officer into the dock. But after that, nothing. So she's on the run, and we have to find her.'

'Where would she go?' Lucas asked softly. 'Does she have a place of safety? Somewhere she can hide out?' He directed the question at Falcon.

'I don't know, but we can check.'

'The letter that was sent to you? Anything there that might just help us locate Fiona,' Loxley asked Lucas.

'Let's have another look at it.' Lucas put gloves back on and took the letter out of its evidence bag. He read it through, then turned to Loxley. 'There's one bit of information at the end that maybe we should follow up on. The reference to looking more closely at the less fortunate in our caring society. Presumably the vagrants.'

'The vagrants again. Whichever way we turn, we seem to come up against the vagrants,' Falcon said.

'So let's see where we are,' Loxley moved in front of a clean whiteboard, and wrote the word PRIORITIES in red marker pen, then sketched in a number of headings.

1 *The CCTV murder.*

'Action: We keep the information that Fiona's no longer in the frame for the murder under wraps for the time being. The Press Office can handle the flow of information to the outside.'

2 *Fiona's place of safety.*

'Action: Question Fiona's friends, that kind of thing. Sergeant, can you co-ordinate that search?'
'No problem, sir.'

3 *Debbie Connelly's regime in the clinic where she and Adam Devine were confined.*

'Action : We need to know how close Debbie Connelly really was to Adam Devine, and if she could have organized anything with him while she was still in that secure environment. Perhaps you can handle that as well, Sergeant?'
'Right,' Goldilocks replied.

4 *The vagrants.*

'Action: Loxley turned to Falcon. 'Gary, take some uniforms down to the docks and start interviewing the vagrants there. I know most of them are off with the fairies, but you never know, we might pick up something.'

5 *The serial killer.*

'Action: We can use your experience here, Carl. According to the first letter a serial killer's been operating in Garton. A particularly nasty example of the kind, apparently. So check out unsolved cases involving potential serial killers, starting with the Garton area. Look for any evidence, however insubstantial at this stage, which might yield a trace on the existence of this serial killer. We'll reconvene at 6.30 this evening.'

As the team dispersed, the atmosphere in the operations centre was considerably more upbeat than it had been earlier.

29

Falcon drove fast as he left police HQ. The call from his father had come in before the next briefing, saying he would be waiting at the same spot in the power station car park. And the low growl of his father's voice had frightened Falcon.

When he arrived it was raining heavily, but his father was standing bare-headed as he leaned against an iron rail above the water, smoking a cigar.

Falcon got out of his car and ran across to him.

'Is it Denise and the kids?' He was panting and made no attempt to hide his concern.

Jeremiah Falcon shook his head.

'No, they're safe.'

'So why this meeting in secret?'

'Lewis knows that he can't reach them. So he turned up the heat on me. From what I was told he's employed a private investigation firm to look into my background. To dig as deep as they could and turn over the old stones.'

'And are there any old stones?' Falcon asked him, more curious than apprehensive.

Jeremiah smiled, a curiously gentle smile. 'Oh, I think we've all got secrets. In your line of business you should know that more than most.'

'Did the people Lewis employed find something in your past?'

For a moment Jeremiah turned away, his eyes drawn to the stark outline of the power station. When he spoke, he kept his face turned away.

'Yes, they found something. Something that happened many years ago. When I was an undergraduate at university.'

'Part of your past where you were a political activist?'

'Yes. I was an activist.'

'But you never denied that. Quite the reverse, in fact. You weren't above playing the revolutionary card if you thought it would help your cause. So what did they find?'

'The answer to a mystery. It was 1970 and I was twenty-one at the time. It was the summer holiday and I went up to London with a group of fellow activists to an anti-racist demonstration. It was at the time that anti-racist demonstrations were just getting started and it wasn't a particularly violent affair. But at the end it turned nasty and when I was coming away I saw a that a gang of four youths had cornered two Asian girls and were starting to attack them. I went to the aid of the girls and their attackers turned on me. One of them was carrying an iron bar and when he came at me I picked up a slab of rubble from the pavement and hit him on the head. He collapsed and the other three members of the gang ran off. I told the two girls to get away themselves and I followed them. Later, I found that the man I'd struck had died.'

'But he was threatening you with an iron bar as you were trying to aid two defenceless girls undergoing a racial attack. Self-defence under the circumstances.'

'Probably. Except for one damning aspect. I panicked and ran away. Leaving the youth to die in the street.'

'Did you phone an ambulance?'

'No, I just wanted to get away.'

'So what did you do?'

'I disappeared into the crowd, and made my way back to the coach we'd come down on.'

'OK.' Falcon was just starting to take in the magnitude of what his father had done. 'So how did the investigators tie you in with the killing?'

'They looked into my past, and one of the things they learned was that I'd been a student anti-racial activist who was "known to the police". But when they looked into those times they came cross something that didn't fit.'

'And what was that?'

'I suddenly stopped being an activist and dropped out of student politics altogether. They found out it was after a particular demonstration in London and they delved into what had happened there and learned about the death of the youth. There was nothing to tie me to the killing. But the coincidence of me finishing as an activist and the youth dying, both associated with the same demonstration, was too strong for the investigators to ignore. So they threatened to send the file they'd built up on me to the Met who would soon find out that my prints matched those found on the slab of rubble that I had struck the youth with. End of story. Unless the evidence has been destroyed, of course.'

Falcon shook his head. 'The evidence may be hidden away in some storage facility out in the sticks. But if this is an unsolved murder it will still be on the Met's books.'

'No more than I expected.'

'So what exactly does Lewis want?'

'The same as when he threatened Denise and the kids. He wants me to persuade my client to retract his evidence. And this time there's no risk of him breaking the law if he exposes me. Quite the reverse, in fact. By identifying me as the person responsible for the death of that youth Lewis would be acting as a "responsible citizen".'

'What do you think will happen if Lewis goes public?'

'At best, I would face a manslaughter charge. But I left that man to die, Gary, and even after all this time the CPS could very well go for murder.'

'Unless you persuade your client to withdraw his testament?'

'Yes.'

Falcon sighed. 'If this gets out the establishment will come after you like the hounds after the fox, you know that?'

'All the enemies I've made defending the criminal fraternity? To say nothing of my anti-racist activities. Oh, yes, they'll come after me, and they'll hang me out to dry. Which is why I'm warning you. It'll get nasty, and you could very easily be caught up in the crossfire.'

30

The team were in the operations room ready to start the evening briefing, and coffee was brought in on a trolley by one of the canteen staff.

'Black for everyone, I think.' Falcon poured out four mugs of steaming coffee, trying to put his father's problems to the back of his mind and concentrate on Fiona. He handed the mugs out as the members of the team settled around the long table.

'So let's take the major lines of investigation,' Loxley said, started the briefing. 'First, any place Fiona could have gone to ground. Sergeant?'

Goldilocks referred to her notebook.

'I started off with Fiona's friends, the *'Three Graces'*. That's a group of three close friends named after Grace Drake who'd brought them together in the first place. There's Grace herself, a children's book illustrator, Hannah Robinson, an up-and-coming lawyer, and Fiona. They all give lectures at the university and they first met at a Vice Chancellor's reception for new staff. Apparently, the three of them hit it off straight away and for the last few years they've met for regular girlie evenings once a week. You know the sort of thing. A work-out in the gym, a massage, a bottle of wine and a take-away, followed by a soppy film. But neither of the other two knew where Fiona was, nor did they have any idea of where she might have gone to ground. It was the same story with Fiona's grandmother Charlotte. The two were very close, but Charlotte didn't know where her granddaughter might be in hiding. In fact, the two friends and Charlotte Nightingale had all learned about the murder from the TV, and were worried sick about Fiona. My contacts were over the phone, so I couldn't see their expressions, but I'd say their reactions were genuine.'

'So they're not hiding Fiona?' Loxley asked.

'I'd say not,' Goldilocks replied.

'What about male friends?' said Loxley.

'The only one I could find was Lance Monkton. He's a professor of Environmental Sciences at the university, but at the moment he's on a scientific cruise in the Arctic.'

'OK, let's move on. What about Debbie Connelly's regime at the clinic?' Loxley asked.

'I spent most of my time on this.' Goldilocks picked up the question. 'Apparently, Debbie was part of a computer-based treatment programme that's been running for the past two years. It's not all that unusual to have online therapy in some types of mental health treatment programmes. But this particular set-up was innovative, and involved patients at four separate clinics talking to each other and to their doctors on a network.'

'Under strict supervision, I assume?' Lucas muttered.

'Yes, everything was password protected. But we now know that Adam Devine spent some time at the clinic, and that he became close to Debbie. So as soon as I learned about the computer network, alarm bells started to ring because it raised the possibility that Adam Devine had remained in contact with Debbie Connelly *after* his release from the clinic. Normally, the password protection security would have been enough to block any attempt by an outsider to get into the system. Except, of course, Adam Devine wasn't any outsider. He was an experienced hacker, and no doubt his expertise far outweighed that of the people running the patient programme. In other words, Adam Levine was in another league. As soon as I learned that, I asked the director, who I'd been talking to, to put me through to the computer technician who ran the programme at the clinic. I explained that we were trying to track down Debbie Connelly in connection with a murder inquiry, and I asked him if it had been possible for her to be in contact with Adam Devine after he'd been discharged back into the community.'

'And?' Loxley prompted her.

'At first, he denied it, saying the security in place was specially designed to prevent out-of-programme contacts. But he finally admitted that Adam Devine had the experience to breach any security that the people at the clinic could build into the system. After that I asked him how the programmes for communication between patients were managed. He said there were cameras for face-to-face meetings, and that the progress of the programme was recorded for each patient on their own memory stick. At that stage I asked him if they still had the memory stick used by Debbie Connelly. When he said they did, I asked him if we could have a copy of the data on it.'

'There was a problem with that, surely?' Falcon came in.

'At first there was, yes. The data was part of a test programme and was highly confidential. I told him I could understand that, but I stressed that this was a murder inquiry. In the end the director compromised, and said that he would allow one of their own technicians to check Debbie Connelly's memory stick. Half an hour later he got back to me. The technician had opened the memory stick and found it had, as expected, data on Debbie's participation in the programme. But he also found something else there as well. There was a second set of data embedded in a hidden file.'

'Was the technician able to access this data?' Loxley asked.

'No.' Goldilocks shook her head. 'He only found the data set because he was specifically looking for it. But access to it was way beyond his capabilities. I asked him then if he could send the "hidden" data here to us. Once he knew the file existed the director agreed to that, and ten minutes later we received a copy of the data.'

'And what was in it?' Loxley again.

'We don't know. But we're working on it.'

31

'While we await developments on the memory stick, let's look at what we picked up from the vagrants. Gary?'

'Not a great success really. We visited the vagrant communities at the north and south dock sites. Not much happening at that time of day, many vagrants just seem to disappear in the light. But there was one thing that did seem to stand out.'

'And what was that ?' Lucas asked.

'There appeared to be an undertone of fear in the communities.'

'Fear of what, exactly?'

'We couldn't tell. But one of the vagrants stood out from the others. At least because he was able to string a few sentences together. And unusually for a vagrant he was happy to give his name. John Carley. Anyway, I brought him back here on the promise of a free meal in the canteen, and he agreed to us interviewing him. I'd already told him we're not treating him as a suspect for anything. You can listen to the interview and watch it through the one-way mirror.'

The man was dressed in a dark overcoat, heavy boots and a trilby, and he seemed to carry a feral odour with him into the interview room. He was accompanied by Falcon who sat him down at a small table. Then the DCI walked over to a tape recorder on a shelf and broke open a pack of tapes. He placed two into the recorder and switched the machine on before sitting down opposite John Carley.

'Witness Statement from John Carley taken on the eleventh of May, 2011. Time, 19 15. Present, John Carley of no fixed abode, and Chief Inspector Falcon, Garton CID. '

'Right, John. Before we start can you state for the tape that you declined legal representation?'

'Yes, I declined.'

'I am obliged to tell you that if you change your mind you can request a legal representative at any time during the interview. Do you understand?'

'Yes.'

'OK, so how long have you been part of the vagrant community in Garton?'

'About six months, I think. Perhaps longer.'

'Why did you become a vagrant?'

Something close to a sigh escaped the man's lips. 'I couldn't face things any longer.'

'What things?'

'Well, my job for a start.'

'What was your job?'

'I was a teacher. Secondary school. Taught English.' He spoke in short, sharp bullet points.

'What was wrong with the job?'

'It was in an inner city area. No interest. No discipline. No learning. The mantra of modern teachers. My wife, Alice, held it altogether for me. But she died.'

He was quiet and tears dropped down his cheek. He blew his nose on a large grey handkerchief. 'I got depressed then and I struck a student in class – an act for which I was sacked. Alice wouldn't have let it happen. But without her, things simply went from bad to worse. Until one day, I just walked away. That was about a year ago, and I wandered around different cities until I settled here.'

'Have you noticed any changes since you first came to Garton?'

'Yes. Like I told the officer at the docks, there's a feeling of fear among the vagrants.

'What are they frightened about?'

'Difficult to say really. They're not the most talkative people at any time. Keep themselves very much to themselves.'

'So you've no idea what caused this fear?'

125

'No, but it seemed to involve something coming out of the darkness.'

'Vigilantes? People who have no time for vagrants?'

' No. I've seen enough of them in the places I've stayed. But not this time. No, this was something else. And there was another aspect to it, as well.'

'And what was that?'

'People started to disappear.'

'From the places where the vagrants congregated?'

'Yes.'

'But surely people come and go in the communities anyway?'

'They do, but I noticed these were gone.'

'Did the other migrants talk about this?'

'Sometimes they did. But most of them are in a fog anyway. They wouldn't know if the sun didn't rise.'

'When did you first notice people were disappearing?'

'Two or three months ago.'

At that moment there was a knock on the interview room door and Goldilocks came in.

'For the tape, Sergeant Maltravers entered the room. She passed a piece of paper to me, and left.'

Falcon read the slip of paper. Then he turned back to Carley. 'John, just one last question. But it's a very important one. Did any of the vagrants connect the fear of things in the darkness with people going missing?'

'Yes, they said a man called the Shadow came and led them away.'

'Why did they call him that?'

'Because he was always in the darkness. Never in the light.'

'Anything else?'

'Oh, yes. Several people who'd caught a glimpse of him said he wore a face mask.'

32

Greg left after lunch to find out what was happening on the outside, and Fiona spent the rest of the day with Petra. The two of them had got on well enough, but as the day dragged out Fiona found herself loosing concentration, presumably a result of the drug residues in her system. In the end Petra had suggested that Fiona lie down for a while.

As she lay in the darkness, Fiona felt tired and dispirited. Depression and low mood: she knew the symptoms well enough. After all, she was a professional.

She traced the string of events in her mind. It had all started with the incident in the glass lift. That was the trigger, and she recognized that she should have agreed to take the counselling that had been offered to her. But she'd coped, hadn't she? Until the next incident when she was found strapped to the fountain in the square. That had reawakened the demons.

But, in truth, other signs had been there. More and more often over the past few months she'd felt she was drowning in melancholy when she thought of the future. She felt so alone, and she had started crying over small irritations. And on top of everything else she seemed to be tired all the time. As a psychologist, she knew well enough that these could be some of the early symptoms of depression, but she'd still refused to seek help. Even though she knew that she could be facing a lonely journey into the barren land that she feared might stretch ahead.

Were there any other symptoms, she wondered? Changes that she'd missed at the time? Or refused to acknowledge?

No, she couldn't think of anything. In fact – and this was important – there were still positives in her view of the world, the biggest being that the symptoms were in their early stages. She knew that because she could still recognize that her thought patterns were sometimes disjointed. She thought of the techniques she'd used on her patients over the years. But she knew the dangers of going down the path of self-treatment. And in any case, right now she was too tired.

Her thoughts began to drift. But she tried to hold onto something positive, hoping it would counter-balance any of the negatives lurking on the edges of her mind. And without thinking she resorted to a coping strategy she'd adopted as a child when faced with anything unpleasant. She forced herself to focus on something good. And without consciously meaning to, she found her thoughts turning to Lance Monkton. But things weren't exactly a rose garden there either. It was, she thought, as if nature was conspiring against her.

Lance was Professor of Environmental Science at Garton University and Fiona had first met him at a reception after he'd given a public lecture under the title *'Looking into the abyss. The discovery of an undersea mountain range.'*

Lance Monkton was a dead ringer for the movie version of the all-action explorer. He had a mass of dark hair and a craggy face with a cleft chin and eyes that always seemed to be searching some far horizon. He had the kind of looks that made him stand out in a crowd. More than that, Lance Monkton had presence.

From that first meeting, there had been a spark between them. But Fiona had deliberately kept him at arms-length, afraid to let him get too close. because she'd soon realized there was a part of Lance Monkton that he kept hidden. It was something in his past, she knew that. But he always clammed up when she'd come anywhere near to that part of his life. As if he'd thrown a fence around it, so that whenever the subject came up he switched moods and almost became another person.

Several times he'd appeared to be about to open up to Fiona. But he'd always pulled back at the last minute.

Until the night that it all came out.

As she lay there, Fiona remembered that last time they'd been out together, the day before he went off on his latest scientific exploration cruise.

The table overlooked the river, the waters lapping against the dock. The candlelight reflected off the cutlery lying on the crisp white table cloth, and the food had been out of this world. Everything set for the romantic evening Fiona had been expecting. And it had been a great evening.

And yet.

It seemed to Fiona that there was an undercurrent that had been there from the moment they'd first sat down. During the meal Lance had been good company, but when the coffee came he seemed oddly nervous and once or twice he appeared to be about to say something.

Finally, he seemed to reach a decision, and the words came out in a rush then.

'Look, I think I'm beginning to fall in love with you. But before we can go any further, there's something you have to know about me. I've never talked about this with anyone, but if we're to have a future you have a right to know.' He sounded almost aggressive.

'Are you going to tell me I have a rival?'

To her surprise he smiled. A rueful, gentle smile that tore at her heart.

'No, you don't have a rival. At least, not in the sense you mean. There was a girl, yes. A very special girl.'

'Then why isn't she a rival?'

'Because she's dead. But she'll always be there. In the background.'

'You mean you can't stop grieving for her? Is that the problem?'

'No, I wish it was that straightforward.' The words seemed to be clawed out of him.

'Then why will she always be there?'

'Because it's my fault she's dead.'

33

For the moment, Fiona was shocked into silence.

'Let me explain,' he said, forcing the words out, 'because if I back off now it might be the end of us.'

She fought down the rush of questions that crowded her mind and let him speak. 'OK, take your time.'

'Her name was Kirsty, and she changed my life. Before I met her I was just another gung-ho climber. I loved the mountains and the wild places. But to me, they had been just playthings. I came to see that through Kirsty. She was Australian and I met her in Nepal when she was doing a round-the-world backpacking trip. She'd just finished a post-graduate degree at Scripps Oceanographic Institute in California. Her speciality was marine biology and the way pollution can affect the evolution of some marine species. I had a post-graduate degree in Oceanography myself, but I'd been more interested in climbing mountains than a career in science. I'd made a couple of films about mountains and climbers, and Kirsty talked me into making marine wildlife films. We started with a number of low budget short films on different aspects of pollution. Then we had a breakthrough, and landed a contract with the BBC to look at how the Antarctic was changing with the onset of global warning. Using the southern elephant seal as a marker.'

'Why the elephant seal?'

'It seems able to cope well with climate change. It needs open water to breed and some marine biologists have suggested that it follows a climate-driven cycle in which it migrates when the open waters move in response to changes in the coverage of the sea ice.

We hoped the animals could be used to predict future changes in sea-ice coverage.'

'So you went looking for the seals?'

'Yes. We knew there were elephant seals on Bouvet Island. It's one of the most remote islands on the face of the earth, over a thousand miles from the nearest land. Most of the island is covered by ice, but there are beaches of black volcanic sand and exposed rock, and it's here the seals congregated. Landing is extremely difficult and Kirsty and I left the ice breaker that was acting as mother ship in a sail boat to explore one of the beaches that looked like a promising habitat for the seals. The beach was an elongated stretch of black sand with an outcrop of rock and sure enough a colony of elephant seals was there, basking in the relative warmth of the sun.'

He paused for a moment, caught in the web of his memories.

'At the back of the beach the land was ice-covered and a glacial tongue extended down to the sea behind the seals. At first glance, it looked a perfect place to film the colony and we decided to reconnoitre the land at the back of the beach before bringing in the camera crew. We landed and secured the sail boat at the end of the beach away from the seals, and then moved up onto the ice above. We were roped together and carried all the right gear, including ice axes and sun glasses. We reported by radio to the mother ship, letting them know what we were doing, then set off up the cliff edge.'

'On the top, we moved along the edge on a traverse that would bring us to a position above the seals. But after about twenty yards we came to a deep crevasse. It was crossed by a number of snow bridges, but we didn't want to take a chance with any of them and we moved further inland to outflank them. And it was then it happened.'

He was silent, looking out of the window into the gathering dusk. But Fiona guessed he wasn't seeing the river in Garton. Instead, he was back in the ice-filled world of Bouvet Island in the remote Southern Ocean.

'The first thing was the noise. A sharp crack that seemed to come from somewhere deep below us. Then before we could react, another crevasse began to open up between our feet, and Kirsty disappeared. And I mean disappeared. One second she was there, screaming as she realized what was about to happen, then she was gone. Lost into the depths of the crevasse. For the moment, I was safe on the side of the abyss as I jammed my axe into the ice in a purely instinctive movement. I could feel the weight on the rope that joined us and I knew that at least Kirsty was still attached at her end.'

His hands shook as he relived the memory.

'The crevasse had opened in response to movement in the glacier tongue, and now the ice started to pull away from the rock over the beach. Below me, the movement caused the ice to groan and tear at itself. Then there was another crack and the sides of the crevasse seemed to come together, almost as if they trying to repair themselves.'

Fiona reached across and gripped his hands, but still they continued to shake.

'The pressure on the rope was enormous by then, and I knew there was little time before the ice axe was torn free. I was already being dragged towards the edge of the crevasse. Nothing could have survived against those pressures. So I cut the rope. To save my own life, I cut the rope. And I killed Kirsty.

'But surely there was an inquiry after the accident?'

'Yes, there was. And I was totally exonerated.'

'But you still blame yourself?'

'Yes.' Just the single word.

Finally it was Fiona who broke the silence. 'It's hard for a girl to fight a ghost. You must understand that. So why did you tell me about Kirsty?'

'I thought we had something, and I wanted you to know the truth. Are you saying I misread the signals?'

'No. You didn't misread the signals. Quite the opposite, actually. But Kirsty was special, very special, and you were right to tell me about her. But she's dead, and you have to exorcise the ghost yourself. Otherwise you don't have a future with me. Or with any other girl, come to that.'

She forced a smile, knowing that it was too dangerous to go any further just then. 'So let's see what happens when you come back from the cruise. But for now, why don't you show a girl a good time.'

And it had been a good time. She was still thinking about that when she finally drifted off to sleep.

34

Loxley turned to Lucas. 'You sent a message to DCI Falcon asking him to put that last question to John Carley. Why?'

The interview with the vagrant was finished and the team were back in the operations room.

'You wanted me to look into the possibility of a serial killer operating in this general area,' Lucas replied. 'Well, I did that, but I couldn't find even the slightest trace of one. But I wanted to know about the vagrant's fear of the darkness, and it seems to be linked to what this character John Carley called the Shadow. A fanciful name, I agree, but the vagrants seem to believe that this person takes them away. And I believed it was worth following up on. That's why I asked the question.'

'Wait a moment,' Falcon came in. 'Just for the record, how many times does a criminal have to commit murder to be classified as a serial killer?'

'No standard answer, but typically, three or more times,' Lucas replied. 'Each murder is separate, but they're linked to the same person by common signatures.'

'Over what kind of period do they operate?' Falcon came in again.

'Usually, at least a few months. But you have to remember there are no hard and fast rules here, and some serial killers are active for far longer perhaps, with extensive dormant periods.'

'And how did you go about looking for traces of a serial killer?'

'Sergeant Maltravers assigned an experienced data handler from her team to the search and we looked for signature murders – that is, murders with features in common – in the region. But we didn't turn up anything over the last year, which is as far as we've got so far.'

'So why the question about the vagrants linking things in the darkness with people disappearing?' Loxley seemed puzzled.

'So far, my publisher has received two letters. In the first letter there was reference to a serial killer. In fact, the appearance of the killer on the board was why I became involved in the first place, to write a book on the investigation that purported to involve one of the most evil serial killers ever to operate in the UK. Then in the second letter we have the hint that the vagrant community may be involved in what was happening here in Garton. Follow this with the vagrants themselves linking the disappearance of members of their community with the Shadow, and for the first time there is a suggestion of a pattern beginning to emerge. Because, when you think about it, a vagrant community offers a serial killer a ready supply of victims that won't be missed by society. And the letters linked the two together: a serial killer and a vagrant community.'

'All right, according to the letter, the serial killer is here in Garton. But in what way is he, or she, linked to Debbie Connelly and Adam Devine?' Loxley asked.

'At the moment, we can't answer that question,' Lucas replied. 'But we think Debbie Connelly and Adam Devine could have been in touch with each other via the computer network when Debbie was still in the secure clinic. So maybe the answers to all the questions will be found if we can open up the memory stick from the clinic. Until then everything remains more or less hidden.'

'So where do we go from here?' Loxley asked, inviting suggestions.

Falcon was the first to come in. 'We have to keep the focus on finding Fiona. But I agree we can't just disregard the possibility of a serial killer operating on the Garton vagrant community either. Not now, after what we've learned about the Shadow. The media would crucify us if it turned out we'd ignored the evidence and let the killer roam the area.'

'Which area?' Goldilocks asked. 'Where do the vagrants actually congregate?'

'I'll show you.' Falcon walked over to a flip chart at the other side of the room. 'We had these maps enlarged for the investigation.'

He turned over several sheets and found the one he was looking for.

'This is a large-scale map of the dock areas.' He picked up a marker pen from the box under the chart, and circled three areas. 'These are the main vagrant gathering points, all in the dock region. One here,' he pointed with the pen, 'in the north of the docks. This one,' he said, indicating another circle, 'is around the caravan drop-in centre. But this area here, in the south, has the biggest vagrant population.'

'I'm impressed. That was quite some off the cuff description of the vagrant areas,' Lucas said.

Falcon grinned. 'The only reason I know anything about the vagrants is that last year we had to deal with a suspicious death among them. And before you ask, no it wasn't the work of a serial killer. Turned out the victim had been in a fight with a fellow vagrant and got his head smashed in.'

'What's that?' Carl Lucas had been studying the map, and he pointed to a green hatched area fringing the south gathering point.

'That's the Waste Land, a derelict area that was due for demolition some years ago. But the funds dried up and the project was put on hold until new funding becomes available.'

'Why was the whole area up for demolition?' Lucas asked.

'The people living there moved out.'

'Because?' Lucas was persistent.

'Because they didn't want to live near the house of a serial killer,' Falcon said.

'Are you telling me that a serial killer has been operating in the area?' Lucas was suddenly alert.

'Yes, the Toy Breaker. But that was several years ago, long before Debbie Connelly and Adam Levine had any connection with the place.'

'But this is weird. Believe me, it's weird.' Lucas started to pace the floor.

'How unusual would it be to have two serial killers operating at different times in the same area?' Lucas asked.

'Independent of each other? Very remote.' Lucas shook his head. 'In fact, I'd say it was on a par with you winning the National Lottery. Unless....'

'Unless what?' Falcon asked.

'Unless we're talking copycat crimes which aren't independent of each other at all. Perhaps the Toy Breaker provided the base for the new killer to operate from.'

Loxley nodded. 'The Toy Breaker's house. A secure base where our serial killer could carry out any murder rituals with little risk of being disturbed. Think about it. Who would go sniffing around a place that was redolent with evil?'

'Jesus.' Falcon suddenly made the connection. 'There's something else as well. Fiona was involved in the Toy Breaker investigation. So, is she also involved in some way with this other serial killer?'

35

'We mustn't forget that the existence of this second serial killer is no more than conjecture based on two things – a vague hint in the letter sent to Carl's publishers and a name mentioned by John Carley.' Falcon pushed the point.

'True,' Loxley agreed. 'But John Carley also said that people have been disappearing from the vagrant communities for months now. But we've no proof of this because no one's been reported missing. And by their nature the vagrants are a mobile community.'

'Wait a minute.' Goldilocks held up her hand. 'It's very difficult to get any concrete data on the vagrants, I agree. But the Social Sciences Department at the University is carrying out a government sponsored research project on homeless communities. The programme was linked with four other universities around the UK.'

'How do you know this?' Loxley asked.

'Because Susan Crompton, who's heading up the Garton input to the programme, came to see me to discuss software that could be used for the study of small-scale population dynamics.'

'Did she discuss the programme itself with you?'

'Not really. It was only in its infancy then. But after the help we gave her, I'm sure she'll be willing to discuss it with us now.'

'Can you contact her, please?' Loxley asked. 'And ask her if she's willing to come to Police HQ and talk to us. Stress that it's extremely urgent.'

Susan Crompton was in her late thirties. She had short dark hair and was dressed in jeans and a leather jacket.

Goldilocks introduced her to the rest of the team.

'Thank you for coming so quickly, Miss Crompton,' Loxley said. 'We appreciate it.'

'That's OK.' Her voice had a soft Scottish burr. 'Sergeant Maltravers told me it was a matter of urgency. And I understand it's about the population survey we've been carrying out among the vagrant communities. So how can I help you?'

She sat down and faced Loxley who lead the questioning.

'Tell us about the survey? What was its purpose.'

'Put simply, to establish the dynamics of vagrant populations. Where the vagrants came from, their background in a society they rejected, their movements, how long they stayed around in one place, and whether or not there was any structure, or hierarchy, in the communities. It was all geared to establishing if the vagrants would benefit from an input to their lives from local government.' She paused. 'That covers the main points, I think. So what is your interest in the homeless?'

'We have reason to believe that several members of the vagrant community at the south dock area here in Garton have disappeared over the past few months, and we're looking for verification. We thought you might be able to help us with that.'

Susan Crompton was suddenly alert. 'What do you mean, you have reason to believe that some of the vagrants may have disappeared?'

'The information came from a source that I can't reveal at present.'

'And this source said that vagrants had gone missing?'

'Yes, and we'd like to know if you picked up any data that might confirm this?'

'Why is it important to the police? They're not usually bothered about the down-and-outs of this world.'

Loxley looked at her, wondering how far he could go. The last thing he wanted was rumours circulating about a serial killer on the loose down by the docks.

'We'd just like to know what's going on down there.' Loxley was fencing, he knew that.

'I see. Well, as a matter of fact what you just said does ring a bell. And yes, we believe from a repeat survey we carried out that at least two or three members of the south dock community have disappeared.'

'How do you know this?' Goldilocks asked her.

'Any vagrant community is difficult to track because the members don't remain static. They're changing all the time. But the community at the south docks does appear to have a core population who have more or less lived there permanently for a number of years. To get some depth into our study we identified five members of this core out of the total population that usually hovered around fifty or so members. That way, we could introduce an element of stability into the overall population. But that was when we hit a problem.'

'What kind of a problem?' Loxley asked.

'At first, we were able to bond to a certain extent with the core members, and everything we picked-up suggested that they would stay around. At least, in the short term. But of the five core members we tagged, two of them disappeared, and in the end we had to change the way we were focussing the survey.'

'Disappeared?' Falcon said. 'Even though some of the vagrants gave the impression that they'd stick around, how could you be certain they would? Couldn't their disappearance simply be because, despite what they said, they've moved on?'

'That's the problem, of course. We can't be sure.'

'Was there any other way in which the survey might be helpful to us?'

'Perhaps. Over the past year or so, the vagrants in the south community have become afraid. Very afraid. They're not the most stable characters at the best of times. But this degree of fear was something else.'

'Who were they afraid of?' Loxley asked.

'I don't think they really knew themselves. But they had a name for it.'

'And what was that?'

'The Shadow.'

36

Goldilocks arranged for a car to run Susan Crompton to the university, and when she came back into the operations room Loxley was summing up the situation.

'So now we have two independent sources, John Carley and Susan Crompton, who have mentioned the Shadow. And as far as the vagrants are concerned, we've freed-up two pieces of information. One, over the last year or so, vagrants have gone missing from their community by the south docks. And two, there's an element of fear among the members of the community. So, the question is, do these facts fit in with what's been happening to Fiona? Or are we dealing with two independent investigations here – one involving Fiona and another involving the serial killer? Carl?'

'Let's see if we can identify any links,' Carl Lucas said. 'Someone's been putting pressure on Fiona, via the incident at the glass fountain and the CCTV murder. And we can definitely tie in Debbie Connelly with the murder she tried to blame on Fiona, because Debbie was identified as the killer from the CCTV images. We can also connect Debbie to Adam Devine, because they had a relationship in the mental health clinic where they were held. And we can connect Fiona and Adam Devine because it was on her advice that he was sent to the clinic. Something Adam Devine blames her for, as evidenced by the threat he made to her.'

Falcon nodded. 'So we have connections between Fiona, Debbie Connelly and Adam Devine as part of an operation to wreak vengeance on Fiona. At this stage, we're assuming that the memory stick will confirm that Adam Devine was actively involved in the plot to harm Fiona as Debbie Connelly's man on the outside?'

'But we have to look more closely at this serial killer,' Lucas said. 'The killer first made an appearance in the original letter sent to my publisher, and since it's reasonable to assume that Debbie Connelly wrote that letter, then there's the connection between her and the serial killer. Tenuous, true, but we can't ignore the fact that Debbie Connelly was responsible for bringing the serial killer to our attention. So, to varying degrees, all the main players are connected. But the big question is, why should Debbie Connelly want anything to do with a serial killer in the first place? The answer, according to the original letter, is that the serial killer was there as bait to bring me into the investigation so I could write a book covering it. True, the book will focus on the hunt for the serial killer, but Debbie Connelly will play a central role in the investigation. Which leaves the outstanding question now of how Debbie Connelly could have conjured up a serial killer, just like that.'

There was a long silence, which was finally broken by Carl Lucas. 'I can't help thinking we're missing something here. Is there an additional link between Debbie Connelly and the serial killer?'

'What kind of link?' Goldilocks asked.

Lucas shrugged. 'I don't know.'

'Additional link, or not, we have to widen the investigation,' Loxley said. 'It's no longer enough just to go after Fiona, because we might have a big time serial killer on the loose in Garton. We more or less put the serial killer on hold earlier, but now they've hit the front.'

'What are you saying?' Falcon asked, suddenly suspicious.

'I'm saying that I have to take this upstairs. I've no choice any longer. And I'm not certain that if push comes to shove Fiona will be our top priority any longer. Not with this serial killer in the matrix.'

For a moment there was a shocked silence. But Falcon had antic- ipated the way Loxley's mind would work. With a big fish like a serial killer in the offing, Loxley wanted the kudos. And Falcon

knew he would have to keep a sharp eye on the superintendent, or
Fiona could easily be side tracked.

Falcon looked at Loxley, and wondered if this was to be the first
locking of horns between them? The first test of strength? But for
the moment he stood back to see what Loxley was actually
proposing.

'Before I take this upstairs, I want the databases checked for any
mention of the Shadow now we know the name.'

'I'll get onto it now,' Goldilocks said.

'How long will it take?' Loxley asked.

'I could do a general search using a few key words in an hour
maybe. '

'Go ahead,' Loxley told her. 'The rest of us will try to map out
our next move, and get something ready to take upstairs.'

As it turned out, Goldilocks was back far sooner than she'd
expected.

'I scanned several police-lead criminal intelligence databases
and carried out a key word search. And I turned up gold after just
a few sweeps, and was able to identify a report of vagrants going
missing in the Newcastle area about five years ago. But the investigation never got anywhere because the community was forever
changing.'

'The same as here in Garton,' Carl Lucas said.

'Right, and I would have dismissed the Newcastle incident for
lack of evidence, but for one thing – the name given to one of the
officers by a vagrant, and later shunted away in a report somewhere.'

'And what was this name?' Loxley asked.

'The Shadow. And there's more, I'm afraid, sir.'

'Now why am I not surprised?' Loxley sounded weary. 'Go on'.

'I can't be certain of this, but it looks as if maybe the attacks on
the vagrants here in Garton and in Newcastle weren't the only
times the Shadow struck. Five years before the vagrants went
missing in Newcastle, there was another suspected attack on
vagrants in Blackpool. The details are too sparse to prove
anything, and there's nothing to link the attacks to the Shadow

except the MO was the same. At least in that it involved vagrants. And if we add in the present spate of missing vagrants here in Garton, to those in Newcastle, it does suggest that someone has had it in for them. In addition, if we bring in the Blackpool attacks, then we can see a pattern in which the Shadow seems to become active after a latent period of roughly five years.'

'A cyclic rhythm,' Lucas nodded. 'Not uncommon with serial killers. They kill and for a while it satisfies their demons. But gradually the stress builds until they can't control it any longer. And that could be what has happened here.'

Before anyone could comment one of Goldilocks's technicians came into the operations room and handed her a memory stick.

'We've got the first documents in clear now. Sorry it took so long to break. But whoever set this up is good. The best I've ever come across.'

37

'My God, there it is. All laid out in front of us.'

Falcon was reading the screen as Goldilocks brought up the decrypted data.

My Darling Lover

I miss you so much now that you have been set free. But the one good thing is that now we can start to take our revenge on Fiona Nightingale, our little princess.

And at the same time you can cleanse your mind again, and release all that tension that has been building up inside you. Now, you will be able to calm your mind. Just think of it, being able to purify your soul again. And just as we agreed, I will direct everything from here, freeing you to carry out the work you were born for.

So become the Shadow again and establish your base in the Toy Breaker's house so that you can live hidden within that dark world. Once everything is in place, you will get your first reward. Just think of it. You will come alive again.

Then when I'm released, we begin the sequence we've been so looking forward to. As planned, we start with the fountain. Then we arrange the episode for the CCTV cameras – just like staging a play really. Once that's done, we draw the little princess into the Waste Land and turn up the pressure on her even further. Then, the final act, when she gets a history lesson – I'm sure she will really enjoy that trip down memory lane. Not.

My darling, I wish with all my heart that I could be with you now, but we knew that when you were released I would have to stay in the clinic until the level of security around me was decreased. The little princess can wait. It may be many months before I can join you, but until then we must feed your demons at the house of the Toy Breaker.

And always remember, the love we have is too strong to falter. And we will be reunited soon, have no fear of that.

Until then be strong, my love, and enjoy the pleasures at the house.

For always, D

'Jesus.' Falcon snapped his fingers. 'There it is. The missing link. Debbie Connelly was connected to the serial killer all the time. Because the killer was Adam Levine.'

'And this.' Lucas sounded almost in awe. 'This is priceless. A blueprint for the actions of a serial killer. Unprecedented access to the core of two evil minds.'

'And it's also a love letter,' Goldilocks said softly. 'From Debbie Connelly to Adam Devine.'

'Yes. And a love letter,' Lucas agreed. 'But even in the passion that runs through every line she's been extremely cautious. No names, no mention of specific events that could stand up as evidence in a court of law.'

'Probably the influence of Adam Devine,' Goldilocks said. 'He must know that however good it is, the security around computer systems can be breached.'

'And we never made the connection between Adam Devine and the serial killer,' Falcon said.

'We had no grounds to do so,' Lucas told him.

'Oh, dear God.' For a moment Falcon stood quite still.

'What is it?' Goldilocks was shocked at the expression on Falcon's face.

'Fiona ran a series of psychological tests on Adam Devine. She suspected something was hidden under the surface, but she couldn't identify it. So after some time in a clinic, incidentally the one where Debbie Connelly was locked away, Adam Levine was released back into the community.'

'So?' Loxley was watching Falcon closely now.

'So, if Adam Devine *is* a serial killer then Fiona could be held culpable for letting him back into circulation, and allowing him to kill again. And Debbie Connelly will use that to humiliate Fiona publicly and professionally. Another massive build-up in the tension level. To add to all the others. And this latest one might just be the final straw to crack Fiona.'

There were a few moments of silence, which was finally broken by Loxley.

'It's apparent now that Debbie Connelly on the inside had been communicating with Adam Levine on the outside in order to take revenge on Fiona.'

Loxley turned to Carl Lucas. 'I asked earlier why did Debbie Connelly need the serial killer in the first place, and you said it was so you would bait to write the book. But we have an additional reason now, don't we?'

'Of course,' Lucas nodded. 'Adam Devine provides Debbie Connelly with a very powerful instrument for tormenting Fiona, and she'll milk the "professional incompetence" card to its fullest.'

'But isn't there a risk that Adam Devine will be caught?' Loxley asked.

Lucas shook his head. 'My guess is that Adam and Debbie will have an escape plan in place. But there is one question we must face right now.'

'And what's that?' Falcon asked.

'Will humiliating Fiona, and getting her locked away as a murderer, be enough to satisfy Debbie Connelly's desire for vengeance?'

There, the question was out in the open now, and Lucas found they were all looking at him.

'She doesn't know Fiona is out of the frame for the CCTV murder, and it would change the whole picture if she did find out. But even as things stand now, the answer to the question is no. Getting Fiona locked away will not be enough to satisfy Debbie Connelly. According to the email, Debbie Connelly has planned a "final act" of revenge. A "history lesson", as she calls it. I think she'll attempt to stage some kind of show. A bit of theatre where she can be centre stage. I believe that's as necessary to Debbie Connelly as killing is to Adam Devine because they both need to have their demons assuaged.'

At that moment one of Goldilocks's technicians came in and handed Goldilocks another memory stick.

'It's a short message this time.'

As Goldilocks exchanged the memory sticks in the computer Falcon asked the technician if the messages could be dated.

'It may be possible and we'll keep working on it but remember, the messages have been encrypted by an expert. We can't even be sure that we've isolated the full content of either of the two messages. And even if they are complete we only have those sent by Debbie Connelly, not the ones she received from Adam Devine.'

'How did that work?' Falcon asked the technician.

'We can't be sure yet, but I suspect that all the communications from Adam Devine self-destructed after being opened.'

'OK, it's coming up,' Goldilocks called out and the rest of the team crowded around her computer to read the second message.

My Darling,

Your last email frightened me. I worry that you seem to be losing the will to strike at the little princess. Please, darling, stay with me. We are so close to our dream now.

To keep on top of what's happening, I have decided to bring everything forward and escape from here in the next few days, so that we can begin the revenge we have planned for the bitch.

I will stay in contact over the net, and I can't wait to see you again, my love

Stay safe.

For always, D

'What's happening here?' Loxley asked.

'I think what we're seeing is the beginning of the break-up in the relationship between Debbie Connelly and Adam Devine,' Goldilocks said.

'I agree.' Lucas nodded. 'We can only see this from one side. From the emails sent out by Debbie Connelly. But I think she believes from the messages delivered by Adam Devine that he was cooling off. And that could make a lot of sense because we know, or at least we're pretty certain, that Devine is a cyclic serial killer with long periods between his killing spells. And he will present a different personality in the two phases.'

'So Debbie Connelly could lose him.' Loxley said.

Lucas nodded. 'It's a great pity we don't have the messages sent from Devine to Debbie because they would have given us some idea of how far the relationship had deteriorated.'

But they were about to get the next best thing when the third letter was delivered.

38

'The relationship had gone far enough downhill for Debbie Connelly to risk escaping from the clinic,' Lucas said. 'And if we believe the emails, it looks as if Adam Devine has been on a killing mission inside the Waste Land – a mission planned with the help of Debbie Connelly which, according to the first email, seems to be centred on the Toy Breaker's house.'

Before they could consider the full ramifications of bringing the Waste Land into the equation, there was another interruption as an officer came into the room. He was wearing latex gloves and carried an envelope addressed to Carl Lucas.

The officer explained that the letter had been delivered to the front desk at Police HQ by a cab driver. Because the envelope was addressed to Carl Lucas, part of the team running the Debbie Connelly investigation, the cab driver had been questioned. He said he'd been waiting in the line of taxis outside Garton Central railway station when a woman asked him to take a letter to Police HQ. She paid him and gave him a generous tip. But all he could remember about her was that she was wearing a long coat with the hood up. When shown a photograph of Debbie Connelly the cab driver had been unable to identify her as the woman who had hired him because she'd kept her face half-hidden under the hood. For the time being, the driver was being held at Police HQ.

Loxley thought for a moment. 'I don't suppose we'll get much more out of him, so get a full statement, then let him go. We can always bring him in if we have to.'

The officer left and Loxley pulled on latex gloves, then slit the envelope and pulled out a single sheet of paper. Like the other two letters, it appeared to have been printed on a PC.

For the benefit of the others Loxley read the letter out loud.

Janus Man. Another letter for your collection. But this time, I feel only sadness. Betrayal is a terrible thing, and can a woman scorned have the strength to carry on? Well, as a matter of fact, yes, she can. I will find that strength, and finish what I started. I will still bring down the little princess. Only now, she will not be the only one to fall.

Go deep into the heart of the Waste Land to the Toy Breaker's house. There you will find the evil. Evil that was only allowed to flourish because our little princess failed to spot a potential serial killer. Someone whose demons can only be assuaged by going on a killing spree.

And I have one more treat for our little princess. She will have a history lesson, and I'm sure she will enjoy her trip down memory lane. And I can tell you, she will visit a truly appropriate place. 'Physician heal thyself', so to speak.

Then I will hand her over to the authorities. She will be a vegetable by then, of course, fit only to spend her remaining years locked away in a secure clinic among the unfortunates of this world.

But, hey, what else does she deserve?

'So there it is.' Loxley broke the silence. 'Carl was right. Debbie Connelly has planned to send Fiona over the edge, then turn her in to us. But by then she'd be reduced to what Debbie calls "a vegetable", which means she will be found unfit to plead in the case of the CCTV murder.'

'Jesus.' Falcon suddenly sounded tired. 'It's such a waste because Fiona's off the hook for the murder. But Debbie Connelly doesn't know that, of course, so she'll go ahead and reduce Fiona to a vegetable. Just as she wrote in the letter.'

'And there's something else in the letter,' Goldilocks said. 'The relationship between Debbie and Adam Devine has finally broken down.'

'So we're not dealing with Debbie Connelly and Adam Devine any longer. From now on in it's just Debbie herself,' Lucas said.

'But why has she directed us to the Toy Breaker's house?' Falcon asked.

'Because that's the hub of what's been happening in the Waste Land. And using the house in the first place was a master stroke,' Lucas replied. 'It was ideal for Adam Devine because no one, not even the drug dealers, would go near it. So he had a secure location where he could assuage his demons, encouraged by Debbie Connelly. And on her part, she had the perfect place to use as a public stage when she arranges to expose the work of a serial killer to the world. But everything went bottom up because Debbie Connelly didn't know Adam Devine was a cyclic killer, so she had no idea that he'd come out of his recent killing mode.'

'And what would have caused Adam Devine to enter this quiescent phase you talked about earlier?' Loxley asked.

'Could simply be he was following a pattern, and was at that part of the cycle where he was resting after the demons had run their course.'

'You mean he would appear to be sane in the quiescent periods?' Loxley asked.

'Oh yes.' Lucas was adamant. 'He would present as a normal member of the community. Until the next time. But right now we have to look at everything in terms of what Debbie Connelly wants, and before we go any further, we have enough now to reconstruct what happened between her and Adam Devine.'

'Go on,' Loxley said, content to let Carl Lucas lead.

'From the very beginning everything revolved around Debbie Connelly gaining her revenge on Fiona Nightingale. Then she met Adam Devine at the clinic where they were being treated, and they found they both hated Fiona Nightingale for shutting them away. It's my guess that it was at this stage that they started to plan their revenge on Fiona. But then something else happened. Something totally unexpected. They fell in love. It must have been then, as they drew closer, that Debbie learned Adam Levine was a serial killer. And then came the great revelation. When Debbie realized that the only reason Adam Devine hadn't been unmasked was because Fiona had missed his symptoms, she must have felt it was her birthday and Christmas all rolled into one. She had the perfect way to publicly humiliate Fiona, and at the same time push her closer to the edge.'

'It would have crushed Fiona,' Falcon agreed.

'It would have shaken her, certainly,' Lucas said. 'So Debbie and Adam hatched their plans. But here Debbie had a problem. She was in love with Adam and wanted to be with him, but she would still be held in the clinic when he was released back into the community. Which meant she needed some way of keeping him on-side when he was away from her direct influence. So she got him to set-up the computer link that would keep them in touch. But I think what worried her most, was learning that Adam felt his demons stirring again. But our Debbie's no quitter, and she turned this to her own advantage and came up with a plan to meet Adam Devine's needs as a serial killer using the vagrants as a source of victims and the Toy Breaker's house as his executioner's cell. Then they put the first part of their scheme into operation when Adam was released back into the community, and he started on a killing spree. But for some reason, Debbie Connelly and Adam Levine fell out of love. Again, it's a guess, but it probably happened as Adam switched to his quiescent mode.'

'You mean he had different personalities, depending on what mode he was in?' Goldilocks asked.

'Could be,' Lucas replied. 'But whatever happened, Debbie was obviously cut up about the relationship falling apart. She'll no longer be able to ride away into the sunset with Adam Devine. But her war against Fiona will still go on. Maybe it will even get more vicious.'

'And will she still use the serial killer on the loose as part of her attack on Fiona?' Falcon asked.

'Absolutely. From her point of view, it's far too good to pass up on.'

'Dear God, just think of the shock that would cause Fiona.' Falcon shook his head. 'A new serial killer using the Toy Breaker's house. A killer who could have been stopped if Fiona had done her job properly. Or, at least, that's how it will appear to the public. But at least one thing's clear now. We don't have to split our forces between rescuing Fiona and trapping a serial killer, because the two strands are joined at the hip.'

'And the Toy Breaker's house is at the centre of everything,' Loxley said. 'So we have no choice now. We have to go into that house. And God knows what we'll find there.'

39

Fiona was tired and felt she could have slept for a week. But something had woken her. Something that had cut through the mist filling her mind. There it was again. Voices raised in anger. One arguing. One pleading.

She remembered where she was then. She was resting. In a house on the Waste Land, where she was hiding with Petra and Greg Harker, the man in the mask. Hiding until it was safe to return to the outside. But now some instinct warned her that she was in danger.

She looked around. She was in a small room, lying on a single bed covered with thick blankets. She was wearing her outdoor clothes, and she remembered being so tired when she went to bed that she barely had time to pull her boots off.

What little light there was in the room came through the open door. From the same direction as the voices. Fiona listened for a while to get her bearings, then swung her legs off the bed and groped around for her boots. When she found them she pulled them on and moved over to the door. Careful not to make a noise she bent down and looked through the crack in the door.

Petra and Greg Harker were arguing.

'It's no good, Greg. I won't leave you here. You say this woman from your past is coming after you, then we'll face her together.'

'You don't understand the terrible mess I've got you into.'

'So tell me.'

He shook his head. 'I can't do that. But I can make sure you're safe.'

'From this woman?'

'Yes, from this woman.' The words were dragged out of him.

'She means you harm?'

'If she doesn't already, she will as soon as she finds out about you.'

'So she's an old girlfriend, is she?'

'She was once, yes. Until I met you.'

'Look, Greg, I can handle past girlfriends of yours. You don't need to send me away.'

'Oh, yes, he does. Don't you, my darling.'

Fiona saw the shadowy figure of a woman emerge from somewhere at the back of the room. She was wearing a long black coat with the hood up. Even in the low light from the oil lamps Fiona recognized her. It was Debbie Connelly. And she was holding a heavy-looking revolver in one hand.

'Do you know what this is?' She raised the revolver. Her voice was soft and mocking. When there was no reply she suddenly pulled the trigger.

The noise of the shot was deafening in the closed surroundings.

'I said, do you know what this is?' She was playing with them now.

'Yes,' Greg Harker replied this time. 'It's a gun.'

'And do I look as if I know how to handle it? Do I?' Debbie's voice was raised now.

'Yes.' Greg Harker sighed. 'You know how to handle it.'

Fiona saw there was something about the way Debbie held the weapon that made her think she certainly did know how to handle it.

'Does that surprise you?' She didn't wait for the answer. 'No matter. Not important, but I was trained in the correct handling of firearms for a part I once had in a play. Only the handling. Not the actual firing, of course. But you'd better worry. Because as you've just seen I know how to take off the safety catch and fire. Bang.'

'Where did you get it from?' Greg asked, and Fiona guessed he was simply trying to gain time.

'From one of your vagrant friends. He brought it out of Afghanistan, but he let it go for a bottle.'

'How did you find us here?'

'I followed the little princess and her minder. You know, the girl who's taken my place. Oh, yes, I was stupid. I trusted my Adam. While all the time he was running wild with you. But he's no guts. He couldn't tell me the truth, could he? He even made up some cock and bull story about having to go away for a few days so he could spend time with me in our hideout without making me suspicious. While you tried to find some way out of this mess.'

'What mess does she mean, Greg? What mess?'

'I'll explain later.' He turned to Debbie Connelly. 'So what do you want?' Adam Devine was beginning to sound desperate.

'What do I want? Let me give you just a tiny little bit of a clue. What about the future we planned together. We had a covenant, the two of us. So where is it now?'

'Let her go. Let Petra go, please.'

'Pretty please? Oh, but I don't think so. NO!' The last word was shouted. 'Not going to happen.'

She moved away so she was directly facing Petra and Greg Harker, and as Fiona leaned forward to keep her in sight she slipped and fell. Debbie Connelly spun round and the gun went off.

Petra fell to the ground gripping the top of her leg.

'Leave her.' Debbie Connelly reacted quickly and stepped further to the side so that she could cover all three people. 'You,' she said, nodding towards Fiona. 'Get over there with the others.'

'Let me look at Petra,' Greg Harker was pleading.

'Quickly. Then back.'

He moved over and knelt by Petra. Then he sighed with relief. 'It seems to have missed the major blood vessels, but it's deep enough to need immediate medical care.' He tried to sound reasonable.

'Not yet. Help her over to the settee. She can lie there until I'm finished.'

Greg Harker lifted Petra and carried her to the large settee in the centre of the room.

'Now, take off your mask.' Debbie Connelly was speaking directly to Greg Harker now.

'Greg?' The other voice was no more than a whisper as Petra began to come round. 'Why does this woman want you take off your mask?'

'So you'll learn the truth about him. See him for what he really is.'

'Greg, it doesn't matter. Show her your injuries.'

'Yes, show us all, Greg. Or she gets another bullet. Now.'

Greg Harker reached forward and ran his fingers across Petra's cheek.

'Sorry, my love.'

He lifted the mask off his face.

'Greg? I don't understand.' Petra was looking at him in amazement, gazing at the clean unscarred skin of his face.

40

'Shocked, are we? Lover Boy's been running a little deception. There's nothing wrong with his looks. Oh, no, it's his mind you want to worry about. Deep down in the black depths where part of him lives. Where the demons are hiding. Demons that little Fiona should have recognized. She could have saved all the killing. But no. She failed didn't she? Lover Boy was too clever for her, wasn't he?' The words poured out in a rage.

'Greg, why the mask?' Petra asked, trying to make sense of what was happening.

'The mask?' It was Debbie Connelly who answered. 'It gives him anonymity, and allows him to move between the two worlds. The Waste Land and the outside.'

Petra tried to say something else, but she collapsed back onto the settee with blood seeping through the fingers of her hand.

At that moment the noise of a helicopter cut through the night. Debbie Connelly cocked her head to the side and listened.

'Damn, the police have started searching the Waste Land. Time to say goodbye, as the song says. You,' she said, pointing the revolver at Adam Devine. 'Pick up the girl. And you.' She turned to Fiona. 'Help him. And please don't be stupid. I have things planned for you, but I'd just as soon shoot you here and now. So move. I want you in the alleyway by the side of the house.'

Adam Devine and Fiona carried Petra outside. In the alley they had to keep to the shadows as the helicopter carried out a grid search of the Waste Land with a searchlight. Debbie Connelly made her captives follow the alley until it opened up onto the main street. Then she directed them to the church. Once there, she forced them to climb the steps. Inside, the building was still lit by the candles around the altar, the light flickering in the draught from the open door.

For a moment, Debbie Connelly paused, looking at the two photographs she'd placed on the steps earlier.

Her and Adam Devine. Fitting then that she'd placed the doll representing Fiona Nightingale between them. Keeping them apart.

But whatever thoughts entered her mind, whatever glimpse she may have had of a future that might have been, Debbie Connelly pushed the images away.

'Over there.' She pointed to a wooden door at the side of the nave. A large pine chest had been pulled across it, and Debbie pointed to it. 'Just a few things I prepared earlier.' She giggled, and that scared Fiona because it meant Debbie was losing her grip. 'Put the girl in a pew,' she snapped at Adam Levine. 'And stay with her, where I can see you both. And you, madam, can earn your salt. Open the box in front of the door.'

Fiona hesitated, but she saw Debbie Connelly raise the revolver and she lifted the lid of the chest. Inside, it had been filled with thick tall candles.

'Drag it across to the centre of the aisle, and leave the top off.'

As Fiona forced the chest across the floor she saw that a can had been hidden behind it. When the chest was in place, Debbie Connelly told Fiona to unscrew the cap on the can and pour the liquid onto the candles. For a moment Fiona hesitated, but the sound of a gunshot echoed through the church and Adam Devine fell on top of Petra holding his arm.

Fiona's hands were shaking almost uncontrollably now, but she did as she was told and poured petrol over the candles.

'Now put the can down and start breaking up the pews. They're rotted anyway. It won't be hard.'

Fiona gripped the nearest pew and pulled on it, then stamped down with her foot. Debbie Connelly had been right. The damp neglected wood snapped away easily enough.

'Stack the wood over the chest.'

Fiona carried on breaking up the pews until the chest was completely covered. Then she was told to pour the rest of the petrol over the broken pews.

'Fireworks now.' Debbie Connelly laughed again. 'It'll be damp with lots of smoke. But we should get a nice blaze when the candles soaked in the petrol lift off. A good diversion for the police.'

'Let me take Petra where she can get help.' Adam Levine had struggled to his feet as he realized what was about to happen.

'All right. But don't you think Miss Perfect from the soup kitchen deserves to know what kind of a man you really are? Don't you?'

'For God's sake, there's no time.'

'So tell her who you really are.'

'What do you mean?' Adam Levine was shouting now.

'I mean exactly what I say. Tell her who you are. It's only fair she hears the truth from the horse's mouth, don't you think?'

'Please, no,' Adam Devine sounded broken. But when Debbie Connelly showed no sign of relenting he sighed and turned to look at Petra. 'I've been responsible for killing people.'

'Oh, but he's being modest. Much too modest. He's a very nasty serial killer. A man that preys on vulnerable vagrants. And when he's satisfied his lust for the kill, he crawls back into society.'

'Damn.' Debbie Connelly cursed as she looked at Petra. 'She's passed out.'

'She needs a doctor.' Adam Devine was pleading now.

The noise of the helicopter came closer across the night sky.

'No time.' Debbie Connelly turned to Fiona and tossed her a box of large barbecue matches. 'Start the fire.'

When Fiona hesitated Debbie Connelly fired the revolver again and Adam Levine's body jerked forward. Debbie Connelly ran over to him and pulled him closer to the fire stack. Then with her free hand she dragged Petra across the floor and threw her on top of her lover, making sure the revolver was aimed at Fiona the whole time.

'What are you doing?' Fiona screamed out the words.

'Letting them go together. Like true star-struck lovers. Now for the fire. But this time I think I should start it. Just to be sure.'

She took another box of matches from her pocket, struck one of the matches, and tossed in into the stack of wood.

The effect was spectacular. The wood started to give off thick smoke as a blue edged flame ran wild. Then the petrol-soaked candles burst into a ball of fire which shot upwards out of the hole in the church roof.

Debbie Connelly pushed the revolver into the small of Fiona's back, and dragged her outside. Above their heads the church continued to burn, throwing hot debris into the air. A side show that lit up the sky, the heat waves forcing the helicopter to retreat.

A heavy mist had come in off the river, cutting visibility to a few yards, and once they were out of the glow of the fire Debbie Connelly guided Fiona in the direction of the chain link fence. Once or twice they had to stop when they heard the sounds of men moving, but eventually they reached it. On the other side the vagrants were sitting around the oil drum, apparently oblivious to the noise of the helicopter overhead or the armed police strung out along the fence at intervals.

As far as Debbie Connelly was concerned, the raid on the Waste Land was unexpected, and when she saw the line of officers, she thought that she and Fiona might have to lie low until the police had gone. But then a disturbance broke out among the vagrants. It was a fight of some kind and at one point the oil drum was knocked over, scattering burning wood over the ground. At that stage the police moved in to control the situation, and Debbie Connelly pushed Fiona through the gap in the fence by the edge of the river. They moved along the shore where they were soon lost in the mist. After a few hundred yards they joined the dock road and came to a small square where Debbie Connelly had parked the nondescript black van she'd hired.

She pushed the revolver deep into Fiona's back, then reached into one of her pockets and pulled out a bunch of keys.

'Open the rear door.' She stepped back to give Fiona space, and when the door was open she pushed her forward. Then she reached inside the van to where she'd previously stashed a syringe.

Fiona saw her raise the syringe, but by then there was nothing she could do as it was driven down into her arm.

Before she drove off Debbie Connelly smiled to herself. 'It's just you and me now, little princess. One on one.'

41

It was a major operation. In the early evening the Waste Land in the south dock area had been shut off and a mobile command centre caravan had been set-up there, alongside the fire appliances and ambulances.

Armed officers were situated at intervals around the chain link fence so that no one could get in or out of the Waste Land. It was a tight perimeter, and when Loxley was happy everything was in place he snapped out a command and mobile search lights were switched on. Then Loxley lifted a megaphone and warned anyone inside the Waste Land to come out with their hands on their heads and give themselves up to the police. The message was strictly aimed at any drug dealers who might be inside the Waste Land. But, when no one came forward, Loxley passed command on the ground to Falcon.

The first wave of police moved forward from their initial positions and entered the Waste Land through the gap in the fence. These were armed officers, together with a designated hostage snatch unit and two dog teams, whose combined job was to sweep the area for any sign of life. To help get their bearings the officers had been supplied with maps prepared by council officials, and were backed up by an officer with a hand-held searchlight. But it was slow work moving from building to building, and when they finally turned into the main street, with its shops and houses, Falcon called a halt to the advance.

He scanned his map with a torch, then turned to DI Logan, his deputy.

'The house we're interested in is just round the corner at the top of the street.'

There was something in Falcon's voice that Logan picked up. 'You not happy with this?'

Falcon shook his head. 'There are buildings on both sides of this street with the potential of hiding an army if necessary. It'll take hours to check every single property, especially since many of them seem to have three floors and a cellar.'

'So what are you thinking?'

'Call up more armed officers to seal off the street, back and front, and move this force straight to the Toy Breaker's house.'

Falcon checked in with Loxley, explaining the problems on the ground, and the new tactics were agreed. When the additional armed men took over the security of the street, Falcon's team advanced and turned the corner.

'There.' Falcon pointed to a crescent of red brick villas that curved in front of a wide pavement dotted with plane trees. 'The house on the far right, with the wall around it. There's a steel gate on the other side but we have the code to open it.'

Falcon led one of the armed units round the side of the wall and paused in front of a gate set into the breeze blocks. But there was no need for the code key because the gate swung open as Falcon pushed it.

'Somebody's been here already. Makes sense I suppose if they've been using the house.'

Falcon edged through the door, flanked by armed officers. Then he stopped and pulled the men around him into a tight circle.

'You can't tell from the outside, but the house was badly burned during the Toy Breaker investigation.'

The house was in darkness now, apart from the single circle of light from the searchlight held by one of the officers – an effect that seemed to heighten the sense of unreality. Slowly the armed unit approached the house, with the searchlight sweeping the section of pavement enclosed by the wall. The front door of the house was boarded up, but on Falcon's orders one of the officers used a claw hammer to prise away the planks that had been nailed across it. They were loosely fitted and came away easily – evidence that someone had tampered with the original security precautions.

As Falcon pushed the door open he caught the smell on the air that flowed from the house onto the street. A strange odour, heavy with a sickly edge to it. A sinister primeval smell. And the dogs tensed.

'Light.' Falcon called for the hand-held searchlight and the officer holding it directed the beam into the lobby beyond the front door. The short lobby had borne the brunt of the arson attack with little of the original floor left. Just the beams, like the ribs of a giant skeleton.

Mike Twist, the inspector in command of the armed response unit, stepped up to stand next to Falcon, his men waiting in line behind him.

'Armed police. Give yourself up,' Falcon shouted, the noise loud in the silence, but there was no reply.

Falcon brought the men and dogs forward, placing them in a semi-circle around the entrance to the house. Then he nodded to Mike Twist and the search of the buildings began.

Ten minutes later Mike Twist came back out. He walked straight past Falcon, almost knocking him out of the way and stood in the street, gulping in the fresh air. One by one his men came out after him, the officer with the searchlight throwing up on the pavement.

Eventually, Mike Twist pulled himself round, and turned to Falcon.

'Never seen anything like that. The cellar's a fucking abattoir.'

Falcon had worked with Mike Twist in the past, and knew he was a tough, experienced officer.

'The smell. I've seen what's causing it.'

'Mike.' Falcon forced a hint of steel into his voice.

'Sorry.' Mike Twist turned to his sergeant. 'Secure the house, all of it, as a single crime scene.' Then he looked at Falcon. 'Do you want to wait until forensics get here?'

'No, I need to take a look now, before reporting back.'

The inspector shrugged and turned back to his sergeant. 'I'm going inside with DCI Falcon this time. But no one else goes through the front door until forensics and the medical team arrive. Let them sort the mess out.'

Then he turned to Falcon. 'You want to see what hell's like, sir. Then join the tour.' He tried to joke, but gave it up straight away.

Mike Twist went first, picking his way across the partially burnt out floor. There were two doors off the side of the lobby and one at the far end by the remains of the stairs. As the men moved forward they passed the first of the doors, which was partially open. Inside, Falcon could see a large pine table with four chairs around it, and a dresser with crockery was against one wall. Everything was covered in a thick layer of grey dust. The second door had jammed, but Mike Twist applied his shoulder to it and it creaked open.

The inside had suffered more damage than the dining room, but traces of family life still remained. Photographs in frames, books and magazines deeply charred in the fire, the remains of a board game on a table by the window. As they passed the rooms with their reminders of everyday family life, Falcon felt a sadness at what the fire had destroyed.

At the end of the lobby, there was little left of the stairs which had collapsed in on themselves, leaving behind a tangle of charred planks. Behind them was a small door.

'The cellar.' Mike Twist stood in front of the door. 'You sure you don't want to wait until Scene of Crimes arrive? Let them go in first?'

'I'm tempted, Mike. Very tempted now we're actually here. But some things go with the job. And I guess this is one of them. So hold the light steady.'

Falcon reached out and held the door knob, then yanked the door open. Even though the armed response unit had opened the door earlier, the air trapped inside was still vile and fly ridden, and Falcon could never remember later what hit him first – the mass of flies which enveloped his head, or the overwhelming smell of corruption that surged from the cellar as the air rushed out.

A flight of steps led onto a stone flagged floor, and the two officers almost ran down them as the flies seemed to go mad in whirlpools of mass hysteria as they were disturbed.

Mike Twist swept the cellar with the searchlight. It seemed to have escaped most of the fire that had enveloped the house. Part of the room contained the tools of the carpenter's trade that the Toy Breaker had used: a long wooden bench, racks on the wall holding rusted tools and a stack of timber in one corner. On the far side of the cellar there was an archway in the brick, and that was where the flies and the smell came from. Before he could change his mind, Mike Twist stepped forward through the arch and Falcon followed.

It was if they'd entered their own private hell.

A thick black wooden beam ran across the ceiling of the cellar. A number of butcher's hooks had been screwed into the beam at intervals, and suspended from them were the naked bodies of three men and two women. All the bodies were covered with multiple wounds, and at their feet a deep channel in the floor had carried away the blood.

But what made the scene even more macabre was the fact that from one end of the row to the other, the bodies were in various stages of decay. And because the degree of decay varied from one corpse to another, indicated by the different life forms which inhabited them, it was like a classroom exercise in forensic science.

And Falcon thanked God that he wouldn't be the one who would have to work the scene.

42

'There was no trace of either Levine or Connelly?' Loxley was in the mobile operations centre, and he put the question to Falcon over the command net.

'No sign of them in the Toy Breaker's house, no. But all the streets are sealed off now. You want us to continue the house to house?'

'I've sent in an additional armed response unit to escort the Scene of Crimes team to the house and safeguard them while they work there. You take your team and the dogs and carry on sweeping the street.'

Falcon gathered his officers around him and was about to starting issuing orders when there was an explosion inside the church halfway down the street and a sheet of flame shot into the air.

Fearful of a trap, Falcon waited until the Toy Breaker's house had been secured by the second armed response unit, then he led his men and the dogs to the gate of the church. It opened onto a paved path that led to a side door in the building. The door was partly open and inside Falcon could see flames leaping in the air. They appeared to originate from a pile of wood stacked in the centre of the aisle.

Falcon stopped and the handlers pulled the dogs back. The heat from inside was intense and Falcon guessed that an accelerant must have been used to start the blaze. He filled Loxley in of developments over the net. 'The interior of the church is ablaze. No way through.'

'You think it's a diversion?' Loxley asked.

'I'd say the fire's a holding tactic as well as a diversion. It's blazing intensely, and the only people who could get into the church now are the fire fighters.'

'Any sign of casualties?'

'No way of telling, not with all that smoke and flame. But if anyone is in there I doubt they'll survive.'

'I'll send a fire engine to the scene and let them take over. What's the state of the fire now?'

'It's already spreading to the surrounding buildings. We can get around the edges, but it will take time. What's on the river side of the church?'

There was a short silence while Loxley examined the map on a plasma TV screen.

'An old quay, abandoned now. We've got the river police launch out, but it can't patrol the whole area.'

'What about the helicopter?'

'Had a problem with the engine, but it should be back up in a few minutes. For now, take your men around the adjacent buildings, and try to seal off the quay because that might be an escape route.'

The fire had already spread deep into the Waste Land, and the best Falcon could do was to come out to the north of the blazing buildings by the quayside and stand around watching as the fire fighters fought to get the blaze under control. At one point, a dog handler radioed in to report that he'd located what appeared to be living quarters. When Falcon led a patrol to the site, he found it was a free standing brick-built garage situated on a plot of land at the back of the shops. The officer explained that the dog had picked up a scent as they'd approached the garage, and when he'd looked inside through a grime-covered window the handler had seen what looked like sleeping bags on the floor.

Falcon moved his men to the garage and sent in an armed response team. When the place was declared secure, he moved inside and shone his torch around. The officer had been right, someone had been living there. And they'd made a conscious effort to make the place cosy. A small trestle table and two fold-down wooden chairs were in the centre of the floor. The table had a cloth on it, with a vase of flowers in the centre. Another small table was against one of the walls, and this one had a primus stove and various cooking utensils and bottles of water on it. The two sleeping bags the officer had seen were on the floor against the opposite wall.

They'd found Debbie Connelly's base inside the Waste Land.

43

Hide from the evil and go where love will protect you. Somewhere safe. That was what her mind was telling her. Offering her a coping strategy. So she closed her eyes and let her thoughts drift.

They were sitting on a rug in front of a crackling log fire, a bottle of wine between them. Comfortable, warm and cosy, the rich red of the wine catching the flames and Myaskovsky's cello concerto playing gently in the background.

Outside, the mist of a mellow New England autumn gave the house a sense of isolation, the two people caught in a world of their own. Fiona was relaxed, partly due to the wine, but mostly because she was happy. More happy than she could ever have expected.

She'd first met Craig when she was working at Deacon Gauter's clinic in the States. One night she'd gone to a party at a colleague's beach house, and there she'd been introduced to a tall, blue-eyed, rangy ex-US Marine. And from that moment they'd hardly been apart.

Craig had a post teaching English Literature at a nearby university. But his great ambition was to be a writer and he already had a successful book of short stories published. The stories were based on his experiences in the US Marine Corps, and the volume had received strong critical acclaim. He was writing a novel when he met Fiona, and that autumn she found a sense of wonder watching the book unfold as Craig wove a tapestry of words around the story. And she remembered other things too. Like the huge pine bed with the heavy duvet that used to fall onto the floor as they made love.

But something was wrong.

She felt it suddenly, and when she reached out to Craig he was no longer there. And someone was talking to her. Telling her he was dead. Attacked by a junkie and left to die on a path through the woods.

She kept her eyes closed, refusing to believe it. But when she opened them again the scene in front of the fire had disappeared, leaving behind an empty shell.

Inside that shell it was dark and cold. Just like the grave. Panic set in then and she started to scream.

But nobody heard her in the depths of that cruel darkness.

She was dragged slowly back into consciousness, and at first she couldn't remember where she was.

But then, for a few moments, her brain achieved a kind of razor-sharp clarity and she remembered being tossed into the back of a black van. She'd struggled, but then she'd felt a stinging pain in her arm and she'd lost consciousness.

Now the questions came in a rush. But her brain was like cotton wool: thick and fuzzy. Try as she might, she couldn't concentrate on any one thing for more than a few seconds. The pain in her arm. She made herself focus on that. She'd been drugged. For a moment, the professional side of her brain switched on, and she tried to work out what drug she'd been given. She thought it could have been Rohypnol again. But she couldn't hold her thoughts together any longer and she started to drift off.

Into the darkness.

When she came around again her mind felt clearer, but all that did was to bring back the panic. Panic driven by the fact that she now realized she was lying rigid in the dark.

Tentatively, she tried to move her limbs one at a time, but they wouldn't budge. What was restraining her? She couldn't tell, and she tried again, and this time she felt some small movement upwards. She strained and kicked, and the amount of slack seemed to increase until eventually her feet clanged against a metal surface. She was trapped in a box. Confined in a metal coffin.

She sensed that this was just the start. And something happened then. A faint flicker of defiance arose in the back of her mind. It had no shape, no form – but it was there, and she was damned if she would go quietly.

She was stronger than that.

44

The team was gathered in the operations room for the morning briefing. And the atmosphere was bordering on despair.

'Anything new?' Loxley didn't sound as if he was expecting anything that would make his day. Or even brighten it up a fraction. But Goldilocks surprised him.

'There's been a breakthrough. I couldn't tell you earlier because the data only came in a few minutes ago. There's a shop called Audio Theatre Systems in the centre of Cresby, a market town about fifteen miles from Garton. The business is a major supplier of sound equipment to the entertainment business on a national scale, and – from what I can gather – they operate from Cresby because the owner likes to live in the country. Anyway, last night the shop was burgled and a range of state of the art PowerPoint equipment was stolen.'

'And this is of interest to us, why?'

'It was reported in to us because we'd circulated a picture of Debbie Connelly to the surrounding forces, and the CCTV footage of the robbery showed a woman who fitted her description. They delivered the footage to us by special courier, and Arthur Fielding's team confirmed that the woman was Debbie Connelly. The camera also caught the vehicle the woman was driving, and they were able to get an index from the CCTV footage. It was registered to a hire firm here in Garton and leased out yesterday to a woman who gave her name as Debbie Connelly.'

'She gave her own name?' Loxley asked.

'She would have had no choice,' Goldilocks said. 'If she wanted to hire a car, she would have had to produce a current driving license.'

'Dear God,' Loxley whispered the words. 'You're right. This is the break we've been looking for.'

'And there was another thing as well.' Goldilocks said. 'Fielding couldn't be certain, but he thinks there was a woman in the passenger seat.'

'What exactly did Debbie Connelly take during the raid on the shop?' Falcon asked.

'Just the PowerPoint equipment,' Goldilocks replied. 'Nothing else, apparently.'

'So what would she want with PowerPoint equipment?' Loxley could have been talking to himself.

'I would have thought that was rather obvious,' Carl Lucas said. 'To present a display.'

45

'No.'

It took a great effort, but she stopped herself from screaming. Breathing. That was it. Concentrate on breathing.

She forced herself to think. How long would the air inside the box last? She had no idea, but all her medical training convinced her that it would last longer if she lay still and kept calm. The problem was, with the drug residues still floating around in her brain, she found it difficult to stay in control of her emotions, much less to keep calm.

Stop it. She admonished herself. Be more positive. Question, who's responsible for this? Answer, Debbie Connelly. There. Not much, but logical thought, all the same.

Next question. Did Debbie Connelly intend to leave her here until the air ran out? She felt the panic rising again at the thought. In frustration she started to kick out at the sides of the box in a blind panic, using up the precious air. Then she drifted off as the drug residues cut in again. As she came back round she found her thought patterns had changed. Strange, but one thing dominated her mind now.

Safety.

It was stupid, she knew that, but she suddenly realized that she felt secure here in the box. Cocooned in a warm womb. She didn't want to be disturbed. That was it. It was as if she no longer had the will to struggle.

In desperation she hacked at the thought, knowing full well that she must not go down that road. The road that led to oblivion. As she struggled to get back in control she realized something was invading her space. Trying to disturb her.

It was the sounds of scraping and scratching. Noises all around her. And the box seemed to be moving. Breaking up her safe secure little world.

Suddenly she felt the sharpness as she dragged cold fresh air into her lungs. And she realized then that the base of the box had moved, but the sides and top hadn't. She was being pulled along on a slide table.

The room was dimly lit, shadows and dark places caught in the glow of a lantern. For a moment she kept still, expecting someone to come to her. But there was nothing. Nothing except silence in the pale yellow sulphurous light. And somehow that was worse. Because she felt detached. As if reality had passed her by. Puzzled, she forced herself to remain as she was, gathering what strength she could from the fresh cold air.

There was still no movement anywhere around her, and in the end she lifted her head tentatively. And what she saw made her gasp. She was strapped to a gurney that stood in front of an open locker set into a wall of lockers.

She was in a morgue.

But something was wrong here. Then she realized what it was. There was none of the sterile cleanliness, and sharp chemical smells, usually associated with morgues. In fact, the whole place seemed damp and derelict, and when she looked closely she could see patches of green mould on discoloured white tiles.

And still no one came for her.

At first, she felt like screaming for Debbie Connelly to show herself and do what she intended to do. Whatever it was. But Fiona was held back by another thought. Debbie Connelly probably wanted her to fall apart. Fiona was determined not to give her the satisfaction and as a first step instead of just lying there, she took the initiative and started to look around.

The first thing she saw was that she was dressed in a none-too-clean hospital gown and slippers. Then she looked at the straps binding her to the gurney, and saw that the strap across her left arm wasn't as tight as the others – almost as if it had deliberately been left that way. She hadn't realized that in the dark, but now if she pulled her hand backwards and forwards she could loosen the strap even more. After a few moments, the rusted fastening snapped and her hand was free. But the effects of the drug were still there, and when she tried to open the rest of the straps her fingers refused to work properly.

She became desperate then. Was Debbie Connelly just playing with her? Was that it? A cruel trick to prey on Fiona's vulnerable state of mind? She felt the panic threatening to come on again. But she lay back and took great gasps of air, filling her lungs and relaxing until she could breathe normally again

Another small victory.

Then she started on the fingers of her free hand. One by one she flexed them, running through the sequence over and over. Slowly, the feeling returned, until she could move her whole hand. Then she turned to her other hand and her legs.

Finally, when she felt ready, she twisted her legs and carefully lowered them onto the floor. She had to wedge the gurney against the lockers so that she could steady herself, but in the end she felt confident enough to take a step. And for the next few minutes she practised walking up and down the room. Beneath her feet there were channels cut in to the floor, presumably to allow blood to flow during autopsies, and a metal table covered with rusted instruments stood next to a door in one corner of the room. Fiona was looking at them, trying to guess their age, when she heard the sound.

The howling of voices reverberating around the room.

The sounds of despair.

46

'To present a display.' Falcon repeated the words. 'So why should she want to run a display? Or, to be precise, why should she want to run a display for Fiona's benefit?'

'One reason only.' Carl Lucas fielded the question. 'To ratchet up the level of stress she's under.'

'What kind of show will she put on?' Loxley asked. 'Any ideas?'

'She's an actress,' Goldilocks said. 'Staging shows comes naturally to her. So what would she want to achieve here?'

'To begin with? Terror.' Lucas didn't hesitate.

'But apparently, she only took the PowerPoint equipment when she carried out the robbery,' Falcon said, 'which means she must have *already* had the material she's going to put on display – material that will provide the show for Fiona.'

'So where would she get that kind of stuff from?' Loxley asked.

'She's an actress.' Goldilocks stressed the point again. 'Maybe she got it from a show she was once in?'

'Good point,' Lucas said. 'We have to check out where she worked before she was sectioned and sent to the clinic.'

'That shouldn't be too difficult,' Goldilocks said. 'If she was in the theatre she must have had an agent who will know all the details of Debbie's career.'

'So how do we find out who the agent is?' Loxley asked.

'We can put Debbie's name into a search engine and see if she has a web page. Many people in the theatre do. It's a way of getting publicity for their wares. I'll check it out now.'

Goldilocks walked over to a vacant computer. It was already powered up and she sat down in front of the screen and keyed in her password. For several minutes material scrolled across the screen, then Goldilocks came back.

'Debbie Connelly maintained a website until about three years ago. But she was only in one production in the year before she was sectioned.'

'What was the production?' Lucas asked.

'"*Visions of Hell*",' Goldilocks answered him. 'It was a TV docudrama – but there's no indication on Debbie's website as to what the subject was.'

'I know *Visions of Hell*,' Lucas said. 'In fact, I was a consultant to the programme, although I never visited the set. But the show has its own website, and it might be worth printing out the background as I think we may have hit pay dirt.'

Goldilocks went back to the computer. It took less than a minute to find what she was looking for, and she printed out a copy of the material on the screen and handed the sheet to Loxley.

'What was it?'

'A TV reconstruction of the treatment handed out to the insane in Victorian times.'

'And Debbie Connelly had a role in this?' Falcon asked.

'Yes, it's shown on the second printed sheet where the full cast is listed. Apparently, she had a small part in the show, and was also a trainee production assistant.'

'What does that entail? Being a production assistant, I mean?' Loxley asked.

Goldilocks shrugged. 'To answer that question in this case we'd have to find someone who was working on the show.'

'But it's possible that Debbie Connelly could have become familiar with the whole production,' Falcon said, 'including how any electronics work – hence the Power Point equipment.'

'Again, we'd have to check with someone on the show.'

'OK. For the moment, leave it. We know Debbie Connelly's got the PowerPoint. So let's move forward from there.' Loxley was fighting his impatience.

'You want me to read out the bit on the first page describing the programme itself?' Goldilocks asked.

'Might save time, sergeant, thank you.'
Goldilocks began to read from the sheet.

'"Visions of Hell", is a reconstruction of life in Cantefal, a large Victorian lunatic asylum, at a period known for the harshness of its treatment of patients suffering mental health issues. The story is based around Mary Grantly, a patient who was admitted in 1855 when she was fourteen for being an illegitimate mother – as were a number of patients in those days. But the baby died at birth and after that, Mary was essentially forgotten by the authorities and left to eke out her life in the most terrible conditions.

From time to time, lip service was paid towards providing Mary with treatment. But the nature of much of this "treatment" was barbaric and involved the use of a number of very odd mechanical restraints, some of them brought in from America by one particular director of Cantefal. Discipline at the asylum was incredibly harsh in that regime, and adherence to strict daily routines was paramount. Cantefal was a terrible place. A forgotten, isolated world that was locked away from society and Mary Grantly's existence was a misery – confined for life in locked wards behind iron railings. All for the "crime" of having a child out of wedlock.

Over the years Mary Grantly changed; she became institutionalized, a dull unemotional personality with her behaviour interspersed with short periods of violence. During these periods she was restrained by a muzzle to prevent her biting staff – a form of restraint already abandoned in many other asylums.

Later, as attitudes changed, life in an asylum became more bearable and patients were put to work as a kind of therapy, and the asylums became self-sufficient in many ways. But Cantefal still remained shut away from the real world. Then an enthusiastic young doctor came to the hospital in the 1920s and exposed the regime. He took care of Mary Grantly as much as he could, and made sure she was as comfortable as possible in her final years.

A TV documentary maker stumbled on the story of Mary Grantly, and saw the potential for a major programme on society's changing attitude to mental health issues.

So far, the programme has won three prestigious TV awards, and it's up for two more in the US.'

'Shit.' Falcon broke the silence. 'A history of the cruel techniques designed to treat mental health problems. It's tailor made to frighten the hell out of Fiona. A horror show dragged from the depths of her own profession. God knows how much Debbie Connelly will make her suffer.'

'Where is Cantefal Asylum?' Loxley asked.

'On the moors above Manchester.'

'We know Debbie Connelly blames psychiatrists in general, and Fiona in particular, for all her problems,' Carl Lucas said, 'and now she's got Fiona to herself – a prisoner surrounded by all those weird treatment machines. I think Debbie's going to put on a special show to take her revenge on Fiona. That's why the PowerPoint equipment was stolen. So she can stage her show at the asylum. And make Fiona suffer.'

'OK,' Falcon nodded. 'Let's assume that Debbie Connelly does intend to put on a show at the asylum. If it was part of her plans, surely she would have made certain that she had the equipment to hand. Picking it up in a robbery at the last minute would have meant leaving too much to chance.'

'I agree,' Loxley said. 'But then we know relatively little of what went on after Debbie Connelly entered the Waste Land following her escape from the clinic.'

'We know one thing,' Falcon came in. 'She had help, and we can assume that came from Adam Devine. Because we found the place where the two of them were living.

'Wait a minute,' Loxley cut in. 'Was there anything found in the love nest.'

'I'll check with the SOCOs,' Goldilocks said, leaving the room. When she came back a few minutes later she was smiling. 'Bingo. A set of PowerPoint equipment was found there.'

'Then why wasn't it reported in?' Falcon asked.

'At first it was hidden, and Arthur Fielding thinks it was protected from any vagrants who might stumble into the hut.'

'So it was there, but Debbie Connelly couldn't risk going back to the love nest, so she had to abandon the equipment.' Falcon was thinking aloud. 'Which meant she had to replace it if she intended to go ahead with the display in the asylum. So why did she break into that particular shop?'

'I think I can guess the reason.' Goldilocks raised a hand. 'The shop was reasonably close to the old asylum, and in her role as a production assistant she may have had dealings with them.'

'We've already covered that, haven't we?' Loxley was beginning to sound openly impatient now.

But Carl Lucas shook his head. 'We haven't even started yet.'

'What is it?' Goldilocks sounded suddenly afraid.

'You have to see this in the original context. Everything Debbie Connelly's been doing has been directed towards putting more and more stress on Fiona. So that when she was eventually caught she'd be unfit to plead for the CCTV murder and get locked away in a mental health clinic. And that would have involved forcing Fiona to change personality.'

'But didn't you say that would have required a trigger of some kind?' Falcon asked.

'I did,' Lucas agreed. 'A massive trigger. And now, thanks to Debbie Connelly, that trigger appears on the board. The shock and the horror that's to be released onto Fiona in the asylum. That's the trigger. And what could have a bigger impact on Fiona than subjecting her to instruments from the dark past of the psychiatrist's trade.'

'Of course, everything changed when Fiona was cleared as a suspect for the CCTV murders,' Falcon said.

'We don't know if Debbie Connelly knows that Fiona is off the hook,' Lucas replied. 'But, and this is the important point, it doesn't matter whether or not Fiona's still a murder suspect. That was the icing on the cake. But Debbie Connelly will go ahead with whatever she's planned against Fiona. Because she still wants her to be reduced to a vegetable state. Debbie Connelly will go on making Fiona suffer until she's broken.'

'But at least that means she'll keep her alive,' Goldilocks said, 'for the moment.'

47

The sound faded. Until it was no more than a faint echo. A trace left behind to hang in the air.

But it stayed in her head. An elusive memory that refused to go away.

She looked around, peering into the shadows as if the source of the howling was trapped somewhere out of sight in that room of the dead. But there was nothing.

Until the spectres came.

They floated in the air above the door. A gathering of women dressed in the uniform of nineteenth century nurses, white caps with red crosses on their heads. Then, like the echo of the voices, the images of the nurses faded away.

Was she in an old hospital, Fiona wondered? The morgue pointed to that. And so did the nurses who'd appeared out of nowhere. But how could all this be happening? She stood there uncertain what to do, then stifled a scream as the light from the lantern suddenly flickered and went out as the door to the mortuary swung open and a draught came in.

Outside, Fiona could see patches of yellow illumination against the darkness and she crossed to the door. As she passed the metal table she picked up a rusty scalpel, gripping it tightly in her fist, then moved out into a wide passageway. Brick arches supported the roof and the floor was paved with stone slabs. In the passage to the right, lanterns had been placed in niches and Fiona edged her way forward, desperate to escape the place where she'd been incarcerated. After a long open stretch, the passageway ended in a brick wall with a wide flight of steps leading upwards into the darkness.

She hesitated at the bottom of the steps, forcing herself to think. She was being drawn forward by the lights. But now she was facing the dark. The unknown. And it frightened her. Then she saw something on the stairs above her.

A woman's face suspended in mid-air. Oh, dear God, Fiona caught her breath. The woman was wearing a metal muzzle. And at that moment Fiona knew she was going mad.

The face hung there, and behind the muzzle Fiona could make out the wrinkled features of an old woman. But it was her eyes that held Fiona's attention, eyes so full of pain and suffering that it was a struggle to look upon them. When Fiona turned away she became aware of something behind the face. It was a string of letters spelling out a name.

Mary Grantly.

For a moment Fiona thought she recognized the name. That it should mean something to her. But the image faded then, taking the letters with it.

A dim glow filtered through the darkness from the top of the stairs. Was the light beckoning again? To show her the way out, this time? Or was the light there to lead her into a trap?

Fiona glanced behind her and as she did so all the lights in the passage went out. Suddenly terrified that the light above would go out as well, Fiona forced herself to climb the stairs. At the top she came out onto a passage. The walls had once been covered in brown painted plaster. But it was mouldy now and damp, and in many places large patches of plaster had crumbled away, revealing the brick underneath. The passage was dimly lit by fluttering lantern light which seemed to be coming out of the walls.

For a moment Fiona stood there, fighting to keep some semblance of control over her emotions. Then she looked around.

A series of arched doorways were set into the walls. The doors to the rooms beyond had been left open and inside the first one Fiona saw a lantern hanging from a hook in the ceiling.

The walls of the room were covered with white tiles, now oozing green slime. At first, Fiona could barely see in the dim lantern glow, but as she approached the door she saw something against the far wall. Fearful of going too far inside a place which could easily become a prison, she strained to see the object trapped in the shadows. And finally she realized what it was.

A restraining chair. A wooden contraption with handcuffs and chains, that had been used in past mental health treatment regimes to immobilise unruly patients who were strapped in it for hours on end. The other rooms also had treatment aids used in eighteenth century mental asylums, finishing with the iconic image of the lunatic asylum – the padded cell, complete with strait-jackets, now crumbled into strips of green mould.

As she moved forward along the passage Fiona realized she was being taken on a journey into the history of the treatment of mental illness. And it was a carefully structured journey, there could be no doubt about that. But how could it be, she asked herself? Who would set up this kind of display? Indeed, who was capable of setting it up? But then the doubts came. Was it a display for her benefit? Or in her imagination was she simply looking at the remains of an old mental hospital, and the rest was no more than an illusion? Perhaps the result of some hallucinatory drug she'd been given?

'That was it.' She hung on to the thought. None of this was real.

Dimly she realized she needed to think. To try and make sense of things. She sat down on the floor of the passage with her back against the wall, and tried to remember what had happened over the past few hours. But then she realized she had no idea whether she was dealing with hours, or days. And try as she may, she couldn't connect with the lost time. Or with any time in the past, come to that.

Who was she? She didn't know the answer, and that made everything somehow so much worse. But she did have the impression that her state of mind was due to taking drugs. OK, she realized that she would have to accept that her memory hadn't come back yet. At least for the moment. And she felt unreasonably proud then. Proud that she'd been able to think with at least some degree of logic.

So, she was in an old mental hospital. But try as she might to regain her memory, it was no good. She kept on seeing the woman in that dreadful muzzle. What was the name in letters around her head? Yes, that was it - *Mary Grantly* .

Was she somehow part of all this?

But no answer came, and the euphoria Fiona had felt a few moments ago dissolved and she was left with a feeling of deep despair and the certainty that she was going mad.

It was then that Fiona started to cry.

'Fiona. Wake up.'

Her head jerked and she realized she must have dozed off.

'Wake up.' The voice again.

She looked around, but in her befuddled state she couldn't work out where the sound was coming from.

Her mind was still all over the place, but she did have a dim memory of sitting with her back against the wall and dozing off. Then someone had lifted her and carried her away. And she no longer carried the rusty scalpel.

'What do you want?' To Fiona her voice sounded raspy.

'Want?' A long silence. 'Yes, what do I want? Do you know who I am?'

'No.'

'Oh, but you will. Before this is over, you will know me. I can promise you that. As you suffer, you will curse my name.'

'Why should you want to—' Fiona suddenly screamed. She couldn't move. She was strapped into the restraining chair.

And a metal muzzle was fastened over her face.

48

'Do you know where you are?' The voice was calm, almost soft.

Fiona didn't answer.

'Oh, well, I'll have to tell you then, won't I? You're underground at the Cantefal lunatic asylum. Do you know why you're underground? Because the barbaric treatment of mental health patients was hidden away in the darkness. And what else can I tell you? Oh, yes, you're sitting in a spinning chair. Do you know what it was for?'

Silence.

'Dear me, we're not very talkative, are we? Then let me explain, although I'm sure you know really. Anyway, the chair was so that patients could be spun around at high speed. Like on a fun fair. Except this was no joy ride. And the treatment didn't do any good anyway. But you know all about treatments that don't do any good, don't you?'

She suddenly moved forward and spun the chair round and round. The effect on Fiona was to bring on an immediate disorientation of the senses. And a deep feeling of nausea.

'Isn't this fun?'

The woman moved forward until her face was caught in the light from the lantern. Fiona saw the features in flashes as the chair spun around. Like that, the face looked as if it was stranded in mid-air behind strobe lights. But Fiona recognized it. The features were etched deeply on her mind.

The *scared* face of Debbie Connelly. And at that moment Fiona's memory came flooding back.

'Did you enjoy that?'

Again there was no answer.

'Well, I'm sure you didn't. But then I don't suppose the patients did either. Anyway, time to move on now. So prepare yourself for the next little treat.'

Debbie Connelly was holding a syringe and when the chair stopped spinning she jabbed the needle into Fiona's arm just below one of the restraining straps that bound her to the chair.

The world was exploding. Bursts of light, like dying stars. And for a moment, Fiona was entranced by their beauty.

Then her eyes opened. But she couldn't move. And the panic rose in her again. She looked around and saw she was standing propped up on a wooden platform over a bath of water. She was naked, and her arms and legs were bound with silver duct tape.

'Let me explain this delightful piece of equipment to you. It's called a plunge bath and it was considered a useful treatment for patients. To shock them into forgetting their illness. How do I know all this, you might ask? I was in a documentary that was shot here at the asylum. Now, are we ready? Go!'

She pulled a lever and Fiona's body crashed down into the bath. The water was icy cold, and the shock to her system made her scream. She thrashed about, but the tape on her arms and legs restricted her movements as the water enfolded her. Debbie Connelly let her thrash around for a few minutes. Then she came up to the bath. She had the syringe in her hand again, and she stabbed Fiona in the arm again.

'Not good for you all these drugs, you know. Goodness only knows what effect they'll have on your mind. But don't worry, because I'll be exhausting my supply before long.'

As she opened her eyes again Fiona vaguely realized she was confined inside a kind of wooden box. She was standing upright, with only her head showing.

'This was a very nasty treatment aid. Patients were confined to the lunatic box when they were violent and needed to be calmed down. Sometimes they were inside for hours, wading in their own excrement. Oh, and one other thing I should point out to you. We can keep you in darkness.'

Debbie Connelly suddenly pulled a short lever and a wooden screen dropped down, plunging Fiona into darkness.

'Oh, silly me.' She opened the screen again. 'We're not finished yet, are we? First, I have to tell you that Adam Devine is the serial killer in Garton. He went back there after he was released from the clinic and started killing again. Five victims were killed because Adam was on the loose. And why was he on the loose, little princess? Can you guess? Oh, I'm sure you can. It was because of your incompetence. You missed his symptoms. So I'll leave you here a little bit, shall I? Let you think about the lives you could have saved. Five people who would still be here. See you later.'

'Was it true?' Fiona asked herself, focussing her mind on that one topic. She had suspected there was something hidden deep in the recesses of Adam Devine's mind. But whatever it was, there was no way it could be teased to the surface. Not at the time Fiona did her assessment of his then current mental state. That was it, she realized it now. At the time she met him, Adam Devine did not display any of the characteristics of a serial killer. It wasn't that she'd missed the symptoms. They were simply not there. She knew she'd done well to identify a potentially dark place in the mind of Adam Levine. The staff at the clinic had much more time to work with Adam, but they'd failed to pick up the danger signs as well. And Fiona realized that Adam Devine was a serial killer with quiet periods. Periods that lasted until his demons emerged from the dark place.

'Oh, I forgot to tell you.' Debbie Connelly was back. 'I've saved the best to last. You're going to have a special experience. A very special experience.'

Her voice took on a sinister sing-song lilt. 'You're going to sample the electric shock equipment used here at the hospital. But it's old and neglected. So who knows what might happen to you? And, dear me, your body's all wet, isn't it. Anyway, I'm going to keep you in the box for a little while to give you time to think about those horrible electric shock machines. Do you know, they've been known to fry patient's brains, leaving behind nothing but a vegetable.'

Debbie Connelly giggled to herself, her fingers gripping the syringe to administer the last drug dose.

49

Fiona felt the terror hit her as she saw the electrical equipment on a rusted trolley that Debbie Connelly was pushing across the floor. Fiona had been drugged again, she knew that. But when she came round she was still in the lunatic box as Debbie Connelly pushed the trolley close.

Fiona forced herself to think. She was free, the duct tape must have been removed when she was unconscious, presumably to allow her movement when she was released from the box. But she was still naked, which made her feel even more vulnerable.

'What did Debbie Connelly intend to do?' Fiona asked herself, then decided that it didn't matter. Whatever happened, Fiona's only weapon against her would be surprise.

For a few precious seconds Fiona let her mind clear, following a technique that she'd learned in the weekly self-defence classes she attended at the gym in the basement of her apartment. Then she focussed on her opponent, willing herself to gather her energy into a ball. And all the time she was telling herself that she was damned if she was going to give in to Debbie Connelly without a fight.

From somewhere she drew on a last reserve, hiding it so she could catch Debbie Connelly by surprise.

'Time to go now.' That sing-song voice rung out again as Debbie Connelly reached forward to open the door of the box. As she did so, Fiona screamed as loud as she could, her voice shattering the silence, and crashed her shoulder against the front of the box. The old wood gave in with a sharp crack, and the door burst open. One of the splinters caught Debbie Connelly in the shoulder and threw her backwards.

It was Fiona's chance.

Pausing only to wrench a wooden plank from the door frame, Fiona went straight into the fight. But Debbie Connelly had time to snatch a long sliver of wood, and for a moment the two figures threw shadows on the wall. Two ballet dancers performing a ritual display.

The plank that Fiona had snatched had a large nail protruding from it, and she used it as a weapon. Once, as they weaved about each other, Fiona caused Debbie Connelly to scream as the nail raked the flesh of her arm. At the start, Fiona was pumping adrenaline around her body in response to the demand for safety. But she'd been forced to take too many drugs over the past few hours, and slowly her supply of energy began to dry up.

The two figures continued their macabre dance, weaving around each other as they sought an advantage. In the beginning, it was a match. Blow for blow. Then Debbie Connelly became aware that her opponent was tiring fast. But Fiona wasn't finished yet, and as she dragged up the last of her reserves one thought kept her going. There was no way she was going to allow Debbie Connelly to win. If she did, Fiona would have to face the electrical shock system. And that realization released one last spurt of adrenaline into her system. At the same time, she remembered what the instructor at the self-defence course had said as he prepared the girls to repel a personal attack.

'You are the victims. In the final analysis all rules are suspended. So play dirty.'

For a single moment Fiona had Debbie Connelly trapped in a corner. And she wound back her arms to *play dirty* and smash the plank into her opponent's face. But as she moved in, she felt her body slowly giving up the struggle, as if it was winding down in a sequence that was out of her control. And she felt herself sink to the floor in front of Debbie Connelly, a lamb to the slaughter.

Debbie Connelly strapped more duct tape around Fiona's body and for the next few minutes she arranged the show she intended to leave behind. When she'd finished she turned to Fiona.

'Do I know how to use this special equipment? It's true that the electrical side of things was Adam's responsibility, and he arranged for us to have a petrol driven generator to supply power to the asylum.'

'He's been here?' Fiona asked.

'Oh, yes, little princess. He came here to set everything in place, and we were supposed to have it ready when we brought you to the asylum. But then Adam ran out on me. I should have known something was wrong, but I was still in love with him. Luckily, I learned how to work the equipment when I was a trainee producer. So, we have power available, but does that mean it will make the electrical shock equipment work safely? You'd better believe it, kid. Otherwise, you'll fry. "Fried Fiona". Has a certain ring to it, don't you think?'

'What about all the drugs you've been using? Where did they come from?' Fiona was desperately trying to gain time.

'Adam got them from a supplier who hangs around the soup kitchen. Anyway, enough small talk. Let's begin, shall we?'

Fiona strained against the duct tape, and tried to scream as Debbie Connelly lifted her unresisting body and dragged her over to a chair she'd placed by the trolley with the electrical equipment on it.

50

Out on the open moor in broad daylight, Falcon felt exposed.

They'd rejected a preliminary helicopter sweep of the area because it would give an advanced warning that someone was approaching the asylum. As the convoy drew nearer to the cluster of buildings, Falcon felt the tension rising in the cab of the Land Rover.

The convoy consisted of a Land Rover in the lead, towing a caravan that was to serve as a Mobile Operations Centre. It was followed by an ambulance, carrying a medical team, and four vans with units of armed police, a hostage snatch squad, and a dog team. A second Land Rover brought up the rear. Loxley, Falcon and DI Dan Logan were in the lead vehicle, and Carl Lucas and Goldilocks in the rear Land Rover. The operation had been planned with as much attention to detail as possible, but Carl Lucas had insisted that Fiona was in grave danger and that time was of the essence.

The hospital lay off the road that crossed the moor. The complex was enclosed within a twenty foot high perimeter wall topped with a bulbous overhang, which was obviously a later edition to the Victorian asylum. There was only one way in and one way out of the hospital grounds, and that was through a gate in the wall.

As the lead Land Rover reached the side turning leading to the hospital, Loxley sent out an order over the radio net to follow his vehicle into the parking area on the open side of the wall. The vehicles drew up in a line against the perimeter fence.

As soon as they were in place, Loxley sent out a recon squad under the command of DI Dan Logan to check the grounds. While that was happening, Loxley gathered the team in the Mobile Operation Centre, and asked Goldilocks to establish a five minute check-in contact with the recon squad. The sergeant sat down in front of a communications console, put on earphones, and called up Dan Logan.

'Control, Superintendent Loxley would like an up-date every five minutes. Anything yet?' For a moment she listened to the reply then she signed off and turned to Loxley.

'Quiet as the grave out there so far, sir.'

'No sign of any vehicles.'

'Nothing reported. And the main gate's still secure.'

'OK, we follow the agreed procedure. First off, securing the grounds – which Dan's doing right now.'

In the operational plan they'd devised, Loxley was to remain in the Operations Centre taking overall command, with Goldilocks running communications and Carl Lucas on hand if needed to treat Debbie Connelly. Once he'd checked and secured the grounds, Dan Logan was to surrender command to Falcon and patrol the car park. Falcon himself would lead a hostage snatch team and a dog team into the asylum.

The operation wasn't nearly tight enough. Loxley and Falcon both knew that, but it was the best they could put together under the time constraints, with getting to the hospital as quickly as possible being the overall priority. But what they wanted more than anything was a plan of the asylum. And for that they had to wait until the fire fighters arrived.

As Loxley stayed in the Operations Centre he knew he had to curb his impatience and let the operation unfold in a structured sequence. The next five minute check-in was on schedule. It just seemed to Loxley to take a long time to come in.

When the check-in was acknowledged DI Logan reported directly to Loxley.

'In the operational briefing we were told that the last time the hospital was officially used was as a film set a couple years ago. Right?' DI Logan asked.

'Yes.'

'Well, it looks as if someone's been here a lot more recently than that. On the far side of the car park there are several patches of oil on the tarmac. We checked them and they looked fresh. They even felt slightly warm.'

'But no sign of the vehicle that leaked the oil?'

'No.'

Loxley thought for a moment. 'So, on the basis of the oil patches it looks as if the asylum's had a recent visitor, or visitors, who used the car park. But there's no sign of the vehicle that was responsible for the oil stain, and nothing to point to an attempted break-in via the main gate. So if anyone was here, how did they get into the hospital itself? Not through the main gate, and they sure as hell didn't shin it over that wall.'

'How long before the fire brigade arrive? Can you check, please?' Falcon turned to Goldilocks.

When they'd planned the operation earlier, Goldilocks had been in touch with the local social services who confirmed that the hospital was the responsibility of central government, but that – for emergency use – a set of access entry codes was logged with the fire brigade. When Loxley got on to them, the senior officer on duty had agreed to take the codes to the hospital. He'd also agreed to supply a fire appliance as a back-up rescue vehicle, but on Loxley's orders it was to be held back until the police operation was underway.

Goldilocks called up the fire engine then turned to Falcon. 'They reckon they're about five minutes away. No more,'

'Thank you. Ask them to go straight to the car park. And no sirens, please.'

The operations centre seemed too small to accommodate Peter Jakes, an imposing figure in his bulky fire fighter uniform and white hat.

He shook hands with Loxley and looked around at the people in the caravan.

'I see you've brought the cavalry.'

'It's one of ours in there, Peter. Or, at least, there's a chance she's in there,' Loxley replied.

Quickly he summed up the situation for Jakes. The fire officer nodded. 'So from the oil stains it looks as if the car park has been used recently, although, as you say, the vehicle, or vehicles, that stopped here have gone now. But they didn't use the main gate for entry to the asylum, and the fence hasn't been breached.'

'Right. So is there any other way they could have got into the hospital grounds?' Loxley asked.

Peter Jakes placed a leather document case on one of the work surfaces and took out a stack of papers. He flicked through them and extracted one.

'This is a leaflet which used to be issued to people visiting patients at the hospital when it was still in operation.'

'Thanks.' Loxley took the leaflet and looked at it. 'What are the different colours for?

'The asylum was due to undergo a series of extensive alterations to meet the present day standards of care for those with mental health issues. They're the areas coloured in green on the leaflet. The only part of the complex to remain untouched was the old asylum itself. It's a listed building on the site of an old monastery and the authorities hadn't decided what to do with it. That's the area coloured red on the plans. But in the end, views on the treatment of patients with mental health problems changed. Large asylums went out of fashion and the whole place has just been abandoned since then.'

Carl Lucas peered at the leaflet. 'Do you know anything about the TV programme that was made here?'

Peter Jakes nodded. 'We carried out a survey to see if the building was safe for the crew to use for the programme, and we had a fire engine on site for part of the filming.'

'Let's presume that the woman we're after wanted to stage something in the old asylum buildings,' Falcon said, 'something that was related to the TV programme. To do that she must have been able to get inside the security wall. So how did she manage to do that?'

'Wait a minute,' Jakes cut in. 'I was called in to advise on safety precautions at one point early in the filming. It turned out that one of the crew had had an accident with a JCB in a corner of the site. Apparently, at one period the inmates of the asylum turned their hand to gardening as occupational therapy, and the garden became a very important part of the grounds. The TV crew were digging a trench as part of a reconstruction of the garden for the programme, when the JCB fell through the ground into a brick-lined passage. It extended to the other side of the wall where it came up in an old chapel in a small wood. It had obviously been some kind of escape route for the monks when the monastery was on the site. The director of the documentary just moved the garden further away and left the passage as it was.'

'This passage?' Loxley asked. 'Was it wide enough to take a vehicle?'

'No.'

'But whoever was here could have left their vehicle in the car park and gained access to the asylum using the old passage. Then driven off when they'd finished,' Loxley said.

'Which, in the absence of the vehicle now, means only one thing.' Falcon had to force the words out. 'Whoever was here did what they came for and are long gone now.'

51

'Maybe they *are* long gone.' Loxley didn't argue. 'But until we know that for certain, we have to assume that, whoever they are, they're still inside the asylum and they're holding Fiona. So we carry on with the operation as scheduled. But first, let's take a look at the plans.'

Loxley and Falcon crossed the floor and joined Peter Jakes who was poring over a plan fixed to a white board with small mounting magnets. For several minutes the three of them studied the layout of the asylum which had two main floors with an extensive cellar area.

'If Fiona is still in the building, she could be anywhere,' Falcon said. 'So I suggest we carry out a systematic sweep of both floors above ground before we tackle the cellars. We could hit everything simultaneously I suppose, but in a building we're unfamiliar with that could lead to confusion. No, I'd rather secure the upper floors first. Then concentrate on the cellars if we still haven't found Fiona.'

He looked at Loxley who nodded. 'Sounds sensible.'

Dan Logan had two units under his command, each with their own leader. Bravo Unit had orders to surround the asylum and secure the perimeter. Once they were in place the main force, designated Alpha Unit, would move into the asylum. Logan would go with them, and a designated officer with a communications set would remain on the steps of the asylum to link the units to the operations centre.

Part of Alpha Unit was a specially trained hostage snatch team. Most of them were armed with Heckler and Koch MP5 submachine guns, but two had sniper rifles. And they all carried tear gas and stun grenades. Other members of the team were responsible for heat-seeking equipment and a variety of other seek and find aids.

When the hospital had been decommissioned the security sequence of inter-locking gates and cages had been shut down, and the main gate now opened directly onto the grounds inside the perimeter fence. Once Jakes had opened the gate, using the keyboard code lodged with the fire brigade, Bravo Unit entered the grounds and took up positions around the asylum.

Falcon went through the gate and looked around to gain his bearings. The main asylum building was directly ahead, with the nurses' quarters and an administration block to one side. Falcon signalled Logan with a hand movement, and the DI sent Alpha Unit forward. Once in position, they began to sweep the walls of the asylum with an infra-red sensor designed to identify body heat. When they'd completed the first circuit of the ground floor, one member of the team climbed a long retractable steel ladder the unit had carried in, and started to check the upper floor. It was slow methodical work and it was over three quarters of an hour by the time Logan sent out the final all clear and reported that there was no sign of life in the two upper floors of the building.

Like the armed response officers, Falcon was wearing a flak jacket. For rapid identification, the jackets carried a broad strip of material that would fluoresce in the beam of a torch. They also wore baseball caps with Police stencilled on them in bright white letters. Once the all clear had been given, Falcon sent two officers back and they escorted Carl Lucas to the front of the building in case he was needed to help Fiona. Loxley stayed in the Operations Centre to co-ordinate the search.

Alpha Unit followed Falcon to the steps leading to the main door of the asylum, keeping together in a tight group. The thick wooden door was closed, but it opened easily enough and Alpha Unit entered the building in a well-practised sequence, covering each other in a chevron pattern. In the pale light from the open door, the ornate entrance hall was a shadowy cavern full of spider webs.

'OK.' Falcon shone a small high intensity torch onto the plan of the seminary he'd brought from the Operations Centre. 'The entrance to the cellars is at the far end of the ground floor. So we make our way there now.'

Falcon would swear he wasn't a particularly superstitious man, but as the unit moved through the asylum he had the impression they were disturbing things that should remain at peace.

Everything led off a long central corridor. The floor was wooden, the planks rotting in places now, but in the torch light it was easy to imagine an army of cleaners brushing and polishing the surfaces. Alpha Unit passed through communal dining rooms, past a laundry with huge copper boilers, into the kitchens, and finished up in a long room full of sewing materials. At one point they entered what was obviously a boardroom, with a large table taking up much of the floor space, and old sepia photographs of medical staff on the walls.

Then they moved through the wards. Row upon row of iron bedsteads covered the floor, and here the sense of something that should be left alone seemed even stronger.

But there was no sign anywhere of an outside presence, and the unit finished up in front of an arch with the steps leading down into the cellars. Two officers carrying submachine-guns went ahead and hugged the walls. Two other men moved past them, their rubber soled boots making no sound on the stone floor. When they signalled the all clear the rest of the unit entered the cellars.

The underground complex had obviously served several functions over the years. A wide passage ran along the spine of the cellars, with water pipes and electric cables on the walls. At intervals, rooms ran off the main passage, and the unit searched each one.

Beyond that section, the cellars appeared to change character, the brick-lined vaults looking much older, as if they were part of an earlier building. After a few yards the passage was blocked off by a heavy wooden door now standing open. On the other side, the light from Falcon's torch showed a narrow passage which opened out into a circular space. Falcon had the lead and suddenly he jerked to a stop, gazing at something revealed in the torch light.

Behind him, the men of Alpha Unit froze into a tableau.

A row of six wooden chairs had been placed in front of a raised stone platform. The chairs were occupied by old women in Victorian clothes, with bonnets on their heads. They sat there, quite still, as if they were waiting patiently for the show on the platform to start.

For the moment, the platform was in shadow, but when Falcon swept it with the torch he caught his breath. A figure was in the far recess of the shadows. It was a young woman dressed in jeans and an anorak, and she was sitting strapped to a tall chair. She had a circular metal cap on her head, connected by a mass of wires to a box on a small table by her side. It was like some grotesque scene from a horror movie in which a mad scientist experiments with the creation of life.

'Jesus.' Falcon couldn't keep the shock out of his voice. 'Fiona wears clothes like that.'

He moved forwards, but as he did so his foot caught a wire that had been run across the floor. And the fireworks started.

There was a series of sharp cracks like those made by ripraps and, one by one, the row of old women in their chairs suddenly came to life. Their limbs began to jerk in spasms and their bonnets caught fire. The girl in the chair was a silent witness to the antics of the women, letting them have the floor.

But when they'd finished she had centre stage for her own show, and it started before Falcon could reach her.

Blue-coloured sparks started to flash between the electrodes embedded in the metal cap on her head, and in response her limbs came to life. It was as if she was being worked by a hidden puppeteer who was putting her through the paces of some frenzied dance.

Then suddenly there was a great flash and the girl and the chair burst into flame with a smell like burning sulphur.

52

'Theatre,' Carl Lucas said. 'Pure theatre. Debbie Connelly must have really enjoyed setting up that little lot.'

They were back in the Operations Centre.

'But where did she get all the gear from?' Loxley asked.

Falcon shrugged. 'We know she stole the PowerPoint equipment, and it's my guess that the mannequins were used to illustrate historical scenes and just dumped when filming finished. I don't know about the fireworks, though. I guess Debbie Connelly, or maybe Adam Devine, must have brought them here.'

'So this was well planned?' Loxley again.

'Oh, yes, very well planned,' Falcon said.

'I agree,' said Lucas. 'Debbie Connelly's a worthy opponent. No doubt about that.'

'So why did she come here in the first place?' Goldilocks asked.

'To torment Fiona on a ready-made stage set.'

'So what do you think Debbie Connelly's next move will be?' Loxley asked Carl Lucas.

'I still believe that at some point, she'll hand Fiona over to the police for the CCTV murder.'

'Just like that?' Falcon sounded angry.

'I doubt it will be just like that,' Lucas said. 'It's my guess that Debbie Connelly's got something planned. Something spectacular that involves a public show.'

'Any ideas what that might entail?' Falcon asked.

'Let's see if we can come up with anything,' Loxley said. 'To begin with, you're sure she'll go public?'

'Yes,' Lucas replied. 'She'll want an audience to witness Fiona's final humiliation.'

'But what about Debbie Connelly herself? Presumably she won't simply hand herself over. So she'll have to leave herself an escape route, and—'

Loxley's mobile phone rang and he removed it from his pocket and took the call.

'Shit.' He cursed as he thanked the caller then put the phone away.

'Bad news?' Falcon asked.

'The worst. Someone's leaked the information to the media that Fiona's no longer a suspect in the CCTV murder.'

'It's another ball game now. With new rules.' Carl Lucas's voice was like ice.

'How do you mean, "new rules"?' Goldilocks asked.

'It was all right as long as Debbie Connelly believed Fiona was in the frame for the CCTV murder. But if she finds out Fiona's in the clear, her options are limited. Either, she piles on the stress until Fiona finally cracks and finishes up spending a long time in a clinic. Or she ends it all by taking Fiona's life.'

'And what's your gut feeling on this?' Loxley asked Lucas.

'Oh, I don't think there's any doubt. She'll take Fiona's life.'

53

The van drove through the night.

It was a short journey to join up with Adam's family, but Debbie Connelly was well aware of the dangers she faced. The main one being that by now the police could have tracked down the van she'd hired, and put out an all points on it. That was why it was vital to reach her destination and ditch the vehicle somewhere it wouldn't be found.

So far, she was aware that her plan to punish Fiona was almost in tatters. And all because Adam had betrayed her. Their future together was now no more than the trace of a dream, and only one thing remained.

Vengeance.

Vengeance against the one person responsible for all her problems: Fiona Nightingale.

For a moment she glanced over her shoulder to the body lying on the back seat. It was a pity the electrical shock equipment had failed to work properly. But when she'd carried out a routine test it turned out that the equipment had been badly damaged at some stage, and the current rushing through it would have killed Fiona instead of just turning her into a vegetable. And that wouldn't do because Debbie Connelly wanted her alive when she was handed over to the police. It was the keystone of her revenge.

So the electrical shock treatment had been used only for the display on the platform, keeping Fiona alive for the final show. A show Debbie and Adam had carefully planned, down to the very last detail. But the master stroke had been down to Adam, with his suggestion that when everything was over they go into hiding with his traveller family who would provide them with transport to safety after the 'little princess' had been publicly exposed for what she was.

Now Debbie would have to hold everything together without Adam. But if she could spin the family some story about Adam joining them later, she might still be able to pull everything off. And one thing was very much in her favour: Adam's family were travellers, and had no cause to love the police. No, all in all, Debbie Connelly felt she would be safe if she could reach them. Safe enough at least to set-up the last show.

To take her mind off things she turned on the van's radio, just in time to pick up the local news.

'Garton police have confirmed that Dr Fiona Nightingale, the forensic physiatrist who was wanted in connection with the so-called CCTV murder, is no longer a suspect in the crime. A full report will follow later in this bulletin.'

Debbie Connelly screamed in frustration. Fiona Nightingale's life was suddenly in great danger.

54

'Apparently, the news has been on the radio and TV, and will make the morning editions of the papers. So we have to assume that it's reached Debbie Connelly, and try and figure out where she's taken Fiona.' Falcon fought to keep down the panic that was starting to wrench at his stomach.

'OK.' Loxley thought for a moment. 'I don't think she'll want to go too far from the asylum because of the risk of being picked up. After all, being on the run isn't easy in these days of CCTV coverage. Especially now that we've put the police on a nation-wide alert for Debbie Connelly, and given out the index of the vehicle she hired. So ideally she wants a location that's public but as near to the asylum as possible. Somewhere where she can take centre stage, in front of a big crowd. Remember, she's had time to plan this. Or, to be precise, she and Adam Levine have had time to plan it. So, any candidates for Debbie Connelly's stage show?'

'Let me surf around a bit. See what's happening locally just now.'

Goldilocks crossed the floor and sat down in front of a computer. Five minutes later she snapped her fingers.

'I've got a possible candidate. There's a horse fair at Paxton, a small market town on the edge of the Lake District, about thirty miles from the asylum.'

'Can you pull up any details?' Loxley asked.

'I can if it has a web page.' Goldilocks put Paxton Horse Fair into the search engine and sat back as the pages scrolled down the screen. After a couple of minutes she printed off a 'History of the Paxton Horse Fair' and Loxley asked her to summarise the data.

'Apparently, it's old, very old, and at one time it was one of the principal gathering places for Gypsies and the travelling community. It's smaller now, but it still brings in several hundred people each year.'

'When is it held?' Falcon asked.

'Now. The fair lasts three days and it's the last day today. '

'Does the fair have any events that Debbie Connelly might try to highjack?'

Goldilocks read through the printout again. 'As well as the actual horse fair, there's a whole variety of side events. Morris dancers, races and sports for the kids, and a genuine Victorian fairground. And on the final day the organisers always put on a show.'

'What kind of show?' Falcon fought to suppress his rising excitement.

'It seems to vary year to year, but it's always linked to the history of the travellers.'

'So, if we get the local force out and use the units from the asylum, we can put together a rapid response search team. Then we take the fair apart – caravan by bloody caravan, if we have to. If Fiona's there, we find her. Just pray we're in time.'

55

It was already dark by the time the convoy from the asylum reached the site of the horse fair.

Loxley had arranged to meet John Liverdale – the co-ordinator of events at the fair – at the site which had been allocated to the vehicles of the police convoy. The convoy was led in by a motor-cycle officer and when the caravan pulled up, Liverdale was waiting for them with a chief inspector from the local force. Falcon ushered both of them into the Operations Centre.

The chief inspector brought the Garton officers up to date. He explained that armed officers and dogs were already searching the horse fair for Debbie Connelly, Fiona Nightingale and the hired van – but with no luck so far.

Liverdale, a short, broad-shouldered, middle-aged man in a waxed coat and tweed cap, turned to Loxley.

'I understand you're expecting some kind of trouble here,' he said.

'Yes,' Loxley nodded. 'How much have you been told?'

'The chief inspector came to see me just now and warned me that the fair might be coming under a threat. Straight away, I assumed he meant a terrorist attack. God knows we have enough of that kind of threat. But the chief inspector explained the police were looking for a female patient that had escaped from a mental health clinic and a woman she was holding hostage.'

'Right. We think the woman may try to hijack part of the show for her own ends.'

'And what might those ends be?' Liverdale asked.

'We're not sure, but we believe the hostage's life may be in danger, which is why we need your help. Can you think of any event she might target?'

'The fair finishes tonight, and there's only one event left: The Fire Ceremony.'

'What's that?' Falcon asked.

'It's an old ceremony that goes back to the pagan days of horse worship. And it's a special performance tonight because it's being filmed for an American TV channel.'

'What exactly happens in this ceremony?' Loxley had to curb his impatience. He wanted to stop the ceremony, but he was aware that blundering in without intelligence could be dangerous.

'It's held on the top of the hill in front of the camp. For health and safety reasons it's divided into a number of individual tableaux, each of which has to pass stringent inspections to meet the regulations. It starts with a ring of fire around the lower slopes of the hill from torches attached to stakes. Then, a silver chariot – drawn by two pure white horses – rides through the ring of fire. Except, of course, the chariot is not drawn by horses nowadays because they'd be in danger from the fires. So it's pulled by two steam wagons dressed overall for the occasion.'

'Does anyone ride in the chariot?' Falcon asked.

'Yes, the "Queen of the Fair", the good spirit that looks after the Earth. She's played by a girl picked each year from the travellers.'

'What happens next?' Loxley was still trying to curb his impatience.

'The chariot pulls up in front of a bonfire that's been laid on top of the hill. It's put together around a thick stake, and at the apex there's a wicker basket with a full size corn dolly inside. The girl gets down from the chariot and does a symbolic dance around the dolly. A dance in which good triumphs over evil. The driver of one of the steam wagons then hands the girl a lighted torch which she tosses onto the bonfire. She then climbs aboard the chariot which pulls back, and when it's clear the driver sets off a firework display by remote control.'

'How big is the display?' Falcon asked.

'It engulfs the whole hillside,' Liverdale replied.

'How long before the ceremony starts?'

'I'm afraid it's already started. About five minutes ago.'

'Are you in contact with the chariot, or the wagons pulling it?'

'We should have had a radio net, but a fault developed and the system's down. The drivers of the chariots have been supplied with mobile phones, but when we checked there was no signal in the hills around here.'

'So they're completely isolated?'

'Yes.'

56

'So let's get this absolutely straight.' Falcon faced Loxley. 'We believe that Debbie Connelly has taken Fiona hostage and is holding her somewhere on the site of the horse fair. She wants to stage a show, so I think we can assume whatever she's planned will be part of the closing ceremony. We don't know which part, so we have to stop the entire ceremony. But we can't reach the wagon drivers. Which means we have to send in an armed response unit to the top of the hill now and pray they get there in time.'

But Loxley didn't reply.

The people in the Operations Centre froze into a tableau staring at Loxley. The superintendent stood quite still, caught in a fog of uncertainty, his limbs rigid.

'Sir.' Falcon forced himself to appear calm. 'We have to get Fiona out before the bonfire's lit and the fireworks start. So we have to get an armed response team to intercept the chariot.'

'But we don't know for certain that Debbie Connelly *is* holding Fiona out there.' Loxley's voice sounded somehow remote.

'But we have to assume that she is. And that she's got something planned for when the bonfire is set alight.'

Loxley looked away. 'In which case, the approach of the armed unit might panic Debbie Connelly into taking action before we can get to her. And with all the fireworks in the area, that could put the armed unit as well as Fiona in danger.'

'I think we should risk snatching Fiona,' Falcon said. 'But we'll have to move now.'

No reply.

'Sir, we have to move, and send the armed response units onto the hill.'

Still no reply.

Falcon looked at Loxley closely. There was a sheen of perspiration on his face and he seemed to have difficulty breathing.

'Right.' Falcon turned to Goldilocks. 'Get me Dan Logan.'

When the DI came over the net, Falcon explained the situation. 'Get the armed response team and the dog unit to the top of the hill as soon as possible. The priority is to rescue Fiona, but first you have to neutralize the bonfire and firework display. Keep me in touch, but you have full command on the ground to react directly to the situation up there. Go for it, Dan, otherwise we think Debbie Connelly's going to make Fiona part of the night's entertainment.'

'Any news on the helicopter?' Logan asked.

'Not yet. It was on another job, and they're sending it here as soon as possible. But we can't wait. We go in now.'

'No.' The voice was strained, but Loxley stood there defiantly. 'We can't send the men in. Not until we have a situation appraisal. Without that it's too much of a risk. God knows what Debbie Connelly's done to the bonfire and firework display.'

'But, sir, the armed unit include a hostage snatch team. They're trained for this kind of thing.'

'Yes, they are, aren't they?' Loxley twisted his hands as the uncertainty in his mind continued to grow.

'And there's no risk to the public because the fire ceremony's isolated on the hill.'

What was wrong with Loxley? Falcon knew a decision had to be made, and he was becoming desperate now as he faced the options. Go over the head of his superior and try to save Fiona, or obey orders and maybe take away any hope of saving her. That was the way Falcon saw it. Black and white. A decision had to be made.

'Sir, we need to move in.' Falcon deliberately kept his tone reasonable.

But Loxley still seemed loathe to act.

'Let me at least send in the hostage snatch team. DI Logan can appraise the situation on the ground, just as you requested, and if the team move into danger he can pull them.'

For a moment Loxley seemed as if he was going to argue but in the end he shrugged and offered no resistance. Instead, he walked to the door of the Operations Centre and went outside.

'Dan, did you pick that up?'

'Most of it, yes.'

'I've taken command, and I'm giving the order. Go after Fiona.'

And there, Falcon thought, goes what's left of my career in the police service.

57

The sound intruded into the quiet of the dark night, single powerful drum beats cutting into the visceral velvet silence. The group was standing outside the Operations Centre caravan as John Liverdale gave a running commentary on what was happening on the hill.

The lights in the camp had been turned down and it was dark. Countryside dark. Then the chanting began. Low at first, but quickly increasing in timbre. And suddenly the darkness was shattered as the strings of lights around the chariot were switched on. The chariot moved majestically up the hill, the girl in white sitting on her throne. And with no lights on the steam wagons, the chariot seemed to float in the air. When it reached the top of the hill, the girl leapt from inside and stood there, outlined against the bonfire. Then she began to dance.

Liverdale caught his breath. 'That's not the dance she rehearsed.'

'Wait a second.' Falcon went back inside the caravan and came out with a pair of high powered binoculars which he handed to Liverdale.

'What about the dress? Is that the right one?' Falcon asked.

Liverdale scanned the hilltop with the glasses. 'As far as I can tell, yes the girl is wearing the right dress.'

'Shit. Debbie Connelly must have changed places with the genuine Queen of the Fair before the chariot started out.'

'So where's Fiona?' Goldilocks asked, a hint of despair in her voice. 'You think we're too late?'

'No.' Carl Lucas shook his head. 'Debbie Connelly needs her

revenge against Fiona to be public. And that could just play into our hands and give us a bit more time. Don't forget, this will be seen on US TV. And Debbie will want her "pound of flesh" to be very public.'

At that moment, Falcon's radio squawked. He flicked to receive and listened.

'Falcon. Go ahead, Dan.'

'We're at the base of the hill. We've just emerged from the trees that the steam wagons came out of, and we're starting to go up the hill. But I have to report we found the body of a teenage girl lying in the trees. She's unconscious with a head wound, but it doesn't seem serious. She's semi-naked.'

'So, it's as we suspected, Debbie Connelly took the girl's dress. And right now she's starting to dance around wicker basket on the hill top. So where's Fiona?'

'Oh, Christ,' Lucas cursed. 'The obvious place. Debbie Connelly must have exchanged her for the corn doll which was in the wicker basket.'

'And Debbie Connelly's going to set fire to it to start the firework display.'

Falcon took the glasses from Liverdale. 'Logan's on his way with support, but look.' Falcon brought the glasses on to the top of the hill. 'The dance seems to be over. The unit's closing, but they won't get there in time.'

'Dan.' Falcon opened the net. 'We think Fiona's in the wicker basket, and Debbie Connelly's going to set it alight. Let the dogs go.'

There were muffled sounds from the hillside and shadows seemed to stream up the hill as the dogs were released. Falcon was watching them when the ringtone of a phone cut through the air, and Liverdale snatched a mobile from one of his pockets. For a moment he listened, then turned to Falcaon and handed him the phone.

'We've got a signal to the chariot, but I don't know how long it will last.'

Falcon took the mobile. 'This is detective chief inspector Falcon.

'That's the wrong girl with the torch. Stop her.' Short, sharp commands, with no time for explanations.

But they were too late, as the driver of one of the wagons had already handed a lit torch to the dancer.

After that, everything seemed to happen at once.

A noise came from the sky. The *thrump, thrump* of a helicopter, and a beam of light fastened onto the hill top.

'Stay where you are.' The amplified voice cut through the night.

But on the ground the dancer held the lit torch.

For a moment, she stood there, a shadow across the hill top. Then she screamed a mouthful of obscenities, and lifted the torch above her head. As she did so, the sound of a single shot cracked through the air. And Debbie Connelly went down. But her momentum pitched her forward and the torch fell on the cage, which burst into flame.

Before the flames had time gain hold, one of the steam wagons drove in front of the wicker basket. The mechanical arm on the front of the wagon had been activated and the driver expertly manipulated it and lifted the wicker cage high into the air. As it swung there, a figure fell out landing with a crash on the ground.

Fiona was bruised but safe.

EPILOGUE

A thin wind came down the estuary, ruffling the surface of the water into short white capped waves.

The two figures walked along the sand by the edge of the sea, flanked by the dog that ran in the water. It was a German Shepherd, an ex-police dog that Mallory had acquired when it was retired. Suddenly it turned and ran back to them, a stick held in its jaws. It dropped the stick in front of Falcon who hurled it back in the water.

'You happy with the arrangements for Denise and the kids?' Mallory asked.

'Keeping them in protective custody until the trial's finished?' We had no choice once we knew they'd been threatened. But I'll be glad when it's all over.'

'We'll all be glad when it's over. How's Fiona by the way? I understand Goldilocks has taken over her care.' For a moment Mallory's eyes glazed over. 'You know, I wouldn't mind her taking care of me. Very attractive, your Sergeant Maltravers.'

'And you married to a vicar. You should be ashamed.'

'Oh, absolutely. But like I say, we can all dream. Anyway,' Mallory continued, changing the subject, 'have the bodies in the church been identified yet?'

'They were in a bad state, but from dental records obtained from the clinic in Cornwall, the male was identified as Adam Devine.'

'What about the girl?'

'We don't know yet, but it seems that a woman from a soup kitchen in the area disappeared at the time of the fire. She was known to have been in a relationship with one of the vagrants, presumably Devine, but we're still checking on her.'

'So it's falling into place?'

'It seems so, yes.'

There was an ease between the two men now.

'But back to Fiona. She's been offered counselling, but she's turned it down because she wants to return to a clinic run by a Father David. She's worked there before, and she feels he can help her. After that, she intends to take a sabbatical year and work in a clinic in New England. She's worked there before and they've offered her a year's contract on a programme they're running on rehabilitation for the most disturbed patients.'

'I'm pleased she's moving forward,' Mallory said. 'We're having her over to dinner this weekend, and no doubt she'll give us all the details then.'

'Debbie Connelly's finally been put to rest. The PCC looked into her death because she was killed by a police marksman but there are no complications because she was about to fry Fiona on that bonfire.'

The dog brought the stick back and pretended not to give it up to Falcon, dragging him along the beach instead. In the end, after the show of strength, it allowed Falcon to throw the stick back into the water. 'Sir.' Falcon sounded uncertain, suddenly wondering if there were certain areas he should steer clear of.

'Yes?' Mallory turned to face him. 'Is this the question you've been studiously avoiding up to now? The question of Superintendent Loxley?'

'Yes, I suppose so. I don't know how much is common knowledge. But there are rumours going the rounds.'

'About his behaviour at the horse fair?'

'Yes, but I had nothing to do with spreading those rumours, I want you to know that.'

'I know you didn't. Your loyalty was never in doubt.'

'Then who grassed him up?'

Mallory's reply was totally unexpected. 'He did it himself. He came to see me the next day.'

'So what will happen now?'

'Clearly, Superintendent Loxley has a problem, and I'm certain he will be offered help to tackle it. An internal board has already been convened, and it will consider his future in the Service. Normally, I don't even think there would have been a board. But there's a smoking gun here, isn't there?'

'Of course, Carl Lucas.'

'He's a journalist, among other things, and he was present when Loxley had his panic attack. We can't afford to go easy on Loxley in case Lucas puts the incident in his book. Hence, the board was convened. Everything shipshape and above board. He'll get a sympathetic hearing, I'm sure. But whether or not he stays in the police may well depend on how long he's known he suffers from panic attacks. If it came out of the blue, OK. But if he was aware that he suffered such attacks, then the board might recommend that he goes. Which is fair enough, I suppose.'

'What has Carl Lucas said? Is he going ahead with the book?'

'Absolutely. He sees this as a once in a lifetime opportunity to report on the hunt for a serial killer from the inside of the investigation that nailed him. So sure, he'll go ahead with the book which will no doubt be a bestseller.'

Mallory whistled and the dog came bounding forward and trotted alongside them as they came towards the end of the stretch of sand.

'One other thing, of course. The other question you've kept away from. Your own future.'

'And?'

'Let me put it this way. Another Promotion Board will be held. No promises, of course, but being second in command on the operation that successfully rescued Fiona Nightingale can't do you any harm. You might find that this time, your star's in the ascendancy.'

Falcon started to relax then. But before he could reply Mallory's mobile phone went off. He took it from his pocket and answered the call.

'Mallory.'

He listened without interruption until the call was finished, and when he looked at Falcon, his expression was strange.

'Problems?' For some reason Falcon suddenly felt uneasy.

'A shock,' Mallory sighed. 'As big a shock as if the seismic plates had shifted under our feet. And if I'm right, from now on things are going to get rough for you. Rough and dirty.'

'Why, what the hell's happened?'

'Fifteen minutes ago your father turned himself in to Police HQ and confessed to carrying out a murder thirty years ago.'